"One of the most fantastic things about Solaria is how little we really know about it. We ourselves were born beneath a region called Aster-space, which is simply that area of space between the concentric shells of Mars-orbit and Asteroid-orbit. We think we know—because the books tell us—that there are smaller shells inside the Mars shell, and greater ones outside the Asteroid shell. What is difficult to accept is that that bare statement is all that anyone on Mars shell actually knows about Solaria. Is it infinite or finite? What lies inside it, and what lies outside? Shockingly, none of us knows.

"I want you to make an expedition right through to the center of Solaria. I want you to see and record every detail, and sort out fact from fiction. I want you to search for the sun which breathed life into human kind. It's a project I've dreamt of for a lifetime, but I would be unable to stand the stress of such a journey. **Therefore you will be my eyes and my ears, ask my questions, and retail my sense of wonder."**

CAGEWORLD SERIES

by Colin Kapp:

SEARCH FOR THE SUN

Colin Kapp

Cageworld 1

DAW BOOKS, INC.
DONALD A. WOLLHEIM, PUBLISHER

1633 Broadway, New York, NY 10019

FIRST DAW PRINTING, SEPTEMBER 1983

1 2 3 4 5 6 7 8 9

DAW TRADEMARK REGISTERED
U.S. PAT. OFF. MARCA
REGISTRADA. HECHO EN U.S.A.

PRINTED IN U.S.A.

CHAPTER ONE

The Lion and Cherry

AS HE moved towards the broad concourse of Hyper-Travel Terminal 211-80-D, many eyes turned in his direction. No one knew him, but many were subconsciously impressed by his physique, by the ease of his movements, and by his engaging ugliness. Had the vast hall been quieter, they might have noticed something even more exceptional about Maq Ancor: he walked as silently as a cat.

Though youthful, his strong face was puckered with a thousand tiny lines, each seeming to reflect an aspect of some considerable intellect. These same lines bestowed on his features an almost animal quality, which, coupled with the mane of red hair which flared over the collar of his cloak, had earned him a legendary nickname. His friends and his enemies—and he had plenty of both—were wont to call him "the Lion". In this they overpraised an extinct beast, for Maq Ancor was more deadly than any creature which had ever lived.

His progress through the various barriers of officialdom was relatively swift. The cost of travelling two hundred and twenty million miles by exospheric liner was a sum more than most men could earn in a lifetime, and therefore traffic on his own flight had been relatively light. People who could afford to make such a journey were normally those with vast resources. The Lion was an exception. His resources were only his skills and his weapons. As an unfrocked master assassin with a staggering price on his head, he was not only unemployed, but dangerously unemployable. Or so he had thought.

His ticket to this destination had arrived together with a set of forged identity documents and other items, and more money than he could have earned in ten years. Its donor was so anonymous that Maq had undertaken the journey nearly a quarter of the way round Mars shell without ever knowing the identity of his patron. His only clue was a pass-book to every item in the Solarian Circus currently playing in the region two-eleven eighty.

5

At the control barrier his identity documents were submitted to the Identifile scanner for verification. Ancor waited for the completion of the process with every outward sign of calm: inwardly, however, he was poised like an animal ready to spring. The documents were forgeries of such perfection that it was difficult to believe they had not been minted by the Solarian Identifile complex itself. But should they fail to pass the computerised scrutiny, Maq was fully prepared to shoot his way out of the terminal.

Shortly the documents came back sealed in the red wrapper of acceptance, and Ancor allowed himself to relax a little. The guards and officials round him never knew how close they had been to sudden death. The examining officer cleared all the paperwork with an air of finality, and appeared to be about to make comment on the high level of armaments carried by one who otherwise had virtually no luggage. Something he read in the lion-face of this formidable visitor, however, made him change his mind, and he opened the barrier instead.

Ancor's route out of the multi-mode travel complex now led him across the main floor of the vast concourse, and here he found it relatively crowded. Long queues were threading towards the vast Spoke-shuttle installation, and there was no eager expectation on the travellers' faces. This was a compulsory emigration centre, and the passenger shuttles only ever went one way— outwards. In order to relieve the crushing pressures caused by an ever increasing population even on a landmass as unimaginably large as that of the Mars shell, it was necessary continuously to siphon off a portion of the people and divert them ever away to where new worlds and new shells were still being created by terraforming. In these wan and tearful queues were those for whom this principle had become the nightmare of reality.

The whole thing was arranged with scrupulous fairness by a computerised lottery which chose those who must emigrate, and which was far beyond any possibility of being manipulated. But the sense of fairness was not reflected in the faces of those torn from their friends and families. Fate—or rather Zeus, the population control computer complex—had dealt their lives a massive blow which most of them seemed to equate with a sentence of death rather than the opportunity for a new and freer life.

The journey would cost them nothing, but it was strictly a one-way ticket. The emigrants' unwillingness to participate was emphasised by the presence of armed guards, who patiently marshalled the frightened and sad-eyed queues, but the imperative necessity for such an operation was underscored by the cybernetic man-seeker engines, controlled directly by Zeus, which patrolled unobtrusively in the background yet were completely deadly in the face of any overt dissension or revolt.

Maq's face hardened as ten thousand envious eyes watched him walking freely away from the terminal. He had taken his own chance in the lottery, and received an irrevocable exemption. None the less he could appreciate the sense of helpless despair in those being herded towards the vast metal maw of the shuttle loading bay. In front of them lay a future they could neither anticipate nor imagine. He wondered suddenly if he was any more sure about what the future held for himself.

By coincidence and at roughly the same time but far overhead, another man was also bound for the Solarian Circus, and was finding his own brand of difficulties about the route. Below him now, Cherry could plainly see the massive sprawl of the circus—mile upon mile of promenade garlanded with necklaces of coloured lights, and with the great opal orbs of the exhibition halls scattered like pearls in a box of brilliant jewels. To the north of the glittering complex, a ring of bright markers outlined the limits of the landing pads, and beckoned his descending craft towards its appointed bay. The very clarity of the scene made Cherry suddenly suspicious. The last time the Solarian Circus had made touchdown he had successfully deceived his rival holo-illusionist, Castor, into attempting to land in a reservoir. Was it now that the trick was being returned?

Having played on this same area of Fed-region two-eleven eighty before, details of the area's navigation beacons were still in Cherry's flight computer. He called them forth to obtain coordinates with which to compare his apparent position, and found the actual location of the circus was nearly two hundred miles to the east. This meant that the grand display beneath him, so convincing from the air, was nothing but a stretch of mudflats and the sea.

Cherry hastily checked his descent and keyed a new heading. The change in the engine note brought his assistant, Carli, out from her cabin to investigate.

"What the hell you fooling at, Cherry? Tez and I have fifty tonnes of projection equipment to unload before we make bed tonight."

"You'd need a submarine rather than a hover-pallet if you tried unloading down there." Cherry directed her attention to the bright panorama. "That's a full ten fathoms of very muddy water."

"That?" She gazed incredulously at the detailed circus scene. Even the little jaunting cars which plied the two hundred square miles of the circus complex could be seen in motion along the promenades; and as they watched, the folds of the great fabric of the 3-D Danse Palace were beginning their reluctant assumption of shape.

"One of Castor's scabby terrain holograms." Cherry's voice was scathing. "Wouldn't fool an infant."

"Well, it would have fooled me," said Carli, unabashed.

Tez, Cherry's projectionist, came up out of the hold to join them. The view brought him a note of admiration.

"That's quite some illusion, Cherry! Luminance balance a bit weak, and some phase-banding from cross-interference between projectors—but what a scale!"

"There's no technique there we haven't already used to better effect," said Cherry disgustedly. "He's just done it bigger, that's all."

Carli sniffed. "Don't recall you ever producing a two-hundred square mile projection, Cherry. Two hundred square yards is about your limit."

"It's the quality not the size which counts, you disbelieving hag! Castor knows it. The rest of Mars shell knows it. So why the hell don't you know it?"

"Because I know you for the crummy fake you really are." Carli ducked the set of navigation indices which Cherry hurled at her, then returned in a more serious mood. "Tell you another thing, Cherry. If you and Castor don't quit fooling with holo-illusions in public places, someone's going to get hurt."

CHAPTER TWO
Holo-illusion and Wheeled Enigma

WITH A true sense of drama, Cherry always chose to give his presentation dressed in a plain white toga and operating from a simple dais in the centre of a bubble hall of neutral grey. This circular arrangement considerably complicated the projection methods, but having mastered his techniques through the years, Cherry knew his presentation was considerably in advance of those of his rivals. Even Carli's introduction was deliberately restrained, and calculated to give the impression that this was to be a very ordinary illusion show. Cherry maintained that such understatements heightened the contrast between his own technical achievements and the works of those like Castor who promised miracles yet produced only the mundane.

As Cherry made his entrance to a modest electronic fanfare he was already studying his audience, quickly identifying several minor illusionists who would be trying to crib points of technique. The majority of the seats were filled with patrons merely hungry for excitement and who had probably hesitated between his own show and the *Mind Daunting Passions of the Twelve Foot Amazons* on the one side and *The Ice Maidens Cometh* on the other.

There was only one figure Cherry could not place. This was one who, incredibly, being fully two-thirds life-support machine and only one-third man, had entered on precise and silent wheels to rest between the most expensive ''inner circle'' seats with a couple of members of a bodyguard or retinue on each side. Despite the man's fantastic disability, his intelligent brow, strong jawline and shattering gaze hinted at some daunting superiority, and the engineering of his body-carriage proclaimed him to be one of vastly more than average wealth. Whoever the fellow was, it was mainly towards him that Cherry directed his bow.

"Friends . . . tonight I take you on a fantastic journey—a journey reaching through to the innermost secrets of the Solarian universe, to visit regions beyond the range of human experience. Imagine, if you will, that the circle which forms the floor of this hall is an observation platform—a vessel uniquely mobile in all possible dimensions. It is to be our vehicle for a trip through domains so fantastic that even reality is superseded."

With a dramatic gesture he pointed his wand at Carli. A great spark flared, and before the astonished eyes of his audience the still-smiling girl became the centre of a great pillar of fire so faithfully projected that it was difficult not to flinch away from the assumed heat. Somewhere a woman screamed as Carli, at the centre of the twisting flame, seemed to melt and begin to drip away like an overheated effigy of wax. Then the flames leaped hungrily higher towards the roof and appeared to ignite the grey translucence of the dome. The cold conflagration ran swiftly across the roof and down the walls to create the illusion that the whole bubble-hall had been consumed by fire, leaving a greatly impressed audience convinced that they were looking straight out at the sparkling panorama of the surrounding Solarian Circus.

To quieten the mild panic which his dramatic opening had evoked, Cherry's voice came calmly from the dais.

"Lo, I, Cherry, bring you illusions more real than reality itself!"

All that visibly remained of the original hall was the circle of white concrete on which the seats were arranged. Now even this appeared to free itself from the ground; and the circus lights, the bustling promenades, and the great exhibition halls fell below in an illusion of swift ascent. Soon the white tablet of the floor adopted an apparently meteoric pace and was heading through the atmosphere, bound for the vacuum of Aster-space.

Swiftly the amazed viewers found themselves high above the surface of Mars shell, soon passing through the great belt of orbiting nuclear-reactor proto-stars called luminaries which heated and lit the surface of the shell, passing one so close that everyone in the audience flinched, imagining that they were about to be fried by its fiery breath. Then the tablet slowed and for a moment appeared poised and immobile, then with a delicious sense of impending disaster, it began to fall back towards the surface of the shell from which it had risen.

Fear of the apparently impending crash sent a little shiver of anticipation through the audience. Many of them sat with clenched fists as they experienced all the visual sensations of hurtling groundward at several thousand miles an hour. There was barely time to resolve the details of the crowded townships beneath before they had "crashed" into the shell itself and were enjoying a welcome period of dark relief before experiencing the sudden returning swoop of light as they broke through the several thousand miles thickness of the Mars shell. Then they zoomed, mazed with vertigo, away from the crowded complexes of the shell's inner surface and up into Aries-space, headed for the "centre" of the universe.

In all this it must be admitted that the form of these latter images was drawn mainly from Cherry's imagination, and that the illustrations were a careful selection of holoscenes captured in other places and at other times. The effect, however, was as convincing as human ingenuity could devise, having regard for the almost total lack of information as to what the centre of the Solarian universe might actually be like.

They traversed Aries-space at a truly heart-stopping pace, flinging themselves into the luminary belt with complete abandon, and were soon descending towards the Earth shell at a velocity which defied belief. Another period of quiet darkness as the Earth shell was penetrated, coupled with the exquisite tension of not knowing precisely when the penetration would be complete. So, with a shock more welcome for its unexpectedness, they soared away from the inner regions of the Earth shell and climbed breathlessly across Terraven-space, headed for the Venus shell.

A similar pattern was repeated for the Venus shell, but now the tension in the audience was visibly rising. Beyond the Venus shell was Hermes-space, leading, so it was said, to the shell and cageworlds of Mercury orbit. Beyond the Mercury shell lay . . . what? Cherry's scenario painted a great black singularity, a remorseless maw which sucked into its terrifyingly voracious trap anything careless enough to enter its domain—including sightseers on a holo-trip. And what lay beyond the singularity? As they were all to be seemingly drawn into this hole to end all holes, Cherry was gratified to hear even some of the male members of the audience begin to whimper.

His descriptive monologue faltered in full flood when he thought his eyes detected at the back of the hall a fleeting silhouette alarmingly like his rival, Castor. Having meticulously built his climax, however, Cherry dared not break the tension by signalling his alarm to Tez in the projection room. With considerable presence of mind the holo-illusionist forced his voice to retain its tone of rising crescendo, yet the quaver which rose in his throat was not entirely the product of the illusion that the tablet of the floor on which they rode was irrevocably trapped by the gravitational attraction of a voracious singularity.

So realistic was the accompanying projection that he knew every member of his audience was mentally bracing himself for the moment when the great radiationless event horizon was breached and they discovered what was contained in the forbidden regions beyond. Knowing Castor's potential for dressing his spite in theatrical garb, Cherry, too, was pierced by a broad shaft of apprehension at the thought of what might happen when the great black orb seemingly swallowed them alive.

Seconds later he found out. As the wave of perfect blackness engulfed them, so a great cyclone draught of freezing air blasted through the interior of the bubble-hall, chilling them all dramatically. At the same instant the power supply failed, and whereas the projectors should now have been picking up with hologram images of Cherry's idea of "otherspace", the darkness remained absolute.

Nor was this all: from the sensation in his eardrums which caused him to swallow frantically, Cherry decided that the cold air injection was being made at a pressure far above that of the atmosphere. Had he intended to introduce physical effects to heighten the illusion, Cherry could scarcely have achieved it more realistically. The trouble was, he had not designed the situation, nor was it under his control.

A woman began to scream with hysteria, seeding an infectious panic which swelled alarmingly as the members of the audience, convinced that something was dramatically out of hand, began to fight their way through the darkness to find the exits. Sweating with apprehension even in the chill atmosphere, Cherry knew their worst moments were still to come. The doors of the bubble-hall opened inwards and had been carefully counterbalanced against normal air pressure. With the rapidly rising pressure inside the hall, there was little chance of the doors being opened without the use of crowbars. Cherry also knew and feared how the impasse would be resolved.

He clung desperately to his lecture console, fighting off the dark mêlée whenever it pressed too close, and waiting for the final blow from the hand of Nemesis. Then it happened: the great bubble-hall, its fabric stressed beyond all reasonable endurance, burst with a sound like the unwinding of the universe. The sudden fall in air pressure was acutely painful to the ears, but it was a pain made welcome by the sudden influx of circus lights as the fabric dome flared open and fell on the startled crowds on the surrounding promenades. Members of Cherry's thoroughly frightened audience shouted with relief at their deliverance, and literally fought each other to be the first to leave by the now over-abundant routes available.

Shortly the house-lights came back on, and Tez, his face bloody from a split on his forehead, peered uncomprehendingly from the projection box at the scenes of ruin below.

"Don't you think you overdid the realism on that run, Cherry?"

"Spool-it!" said Cherry wearily. "Wait till I get my hands on that rat-faced runt Castor. That must be the lousiest stinking trick he ever pulled. I'll shake that old skeleton until his eyeballs rattle in their sockets."

Hearing a sudden noise behind him, Cherry looked round, aware for the first time that a small proportion of his audience had remained. The imperious stranger, half-man, half-machine, was still waiting impassively between his bodyguards, looking as though he had detected nothing untoward about the events of the past few minutes. He beckoned the perplexed Cherry to come towards him.

"That was a very impressive and imaginative performance, Magician Cherry." The timbre of the man's voice fully matched his outer signs of superiority. "Suffice it to say that your conception of the Solarian universe is utterly wrong, but you have good mastery of the magicians' craft. I thought the ending was particularly unforgettable.''

"I don't think I'll forget it in a hurry, either," said Cherry unhappily. "It wasn't supposed to end like that. I was sabotaged.''

"Nonetheless I was able to verify what my researches had already told me about your proficiency with holo-illusions. Soon I think we shall talk some more. I shall have a proposition for you.''

"I would welcome the opportunity to be of service," said Cherry in his silkiest tone. "By what name should I know my patron?''

"They call me Land-a." The merest movement of the stranger's finger was the sign for one of the bodyguards to pass Cherry a card with a legend seemingly written in silver wire pressed flush into the whiteness of its surface. Cherry scanned it, but could decipher only the fact that it was written in a non-Federation language which he did not know. He was about to ask for clarification when the stranger wheeled about abruptly, and with his retinue deployed expertly on either side, ran swiftly and smoothly from the ruins of the hall.

Still holding the white card, Cherry had watched the wheeled enigma depart, wondering what manner of proposition such a man would offer a circus illusionist. His reverie was shattered by the arrival of Chi Nailer, the circus-marshal, with his disaster team. Despite the grim lines on Nailer's face, his eyes were awash with an amusement too powerful for suppression.

"You've really excelled yourself this time, Cherry! I've known you to pull some crazy tricks before, but actually bursting a bubble-hall is the wildest yet. How the hell did you manage it?''

"I was sabotaged. At a guess somebody connected us up to a circus pressure main. To judge from the temperature drop, what we actually received was intended for the ice-maidens next door.''

Chi Nailer walked moodily through the torn folds of bubble fabric to examine the area where the great flexible pipes of the circus service mains ran untidily along the surface of the sand. The illusionist's guess was proved a fact beyond doubt—a pressure manifold had indeed been coupled to the input of Cherry's fan.

Nailer grimaced. "I can see what was done, but I don't see how it was done. It must have taken the best part of half an hour to adapt that manifold. How come nobody saw it?''

"No problem," said Cherry. "Kill that big overhead light

over there, then flood the whole area with a terrain hologram of the same scene but projected about a metre higher. You could work underneath the projected image any length of time and nobody would ever know you were there."

"Which expert knowledge suggests Castor was responsible. This vendetta of yours is becoming a public menace. My disaster team has better things to do than attend crises you've manufactured for each other. I'll give you fair warning, Cherry—if there's one more incident like this whilst you're under circus jurisdiction, I'll personally guarantee you'll neither of you ever work in a circus again. Is that perfectly clear?"

"Do me a favour, Chi. Allow me one last crack at that rat-faced buzzard—just to even up the score."

"You've had your warning!" Nailer called his team together and listened to a summary of their reports. Then he indicated the ruins of the bubble-hall. "And you'd better get this lot cleared fast, Cherry. Gives the circus a bad image."

"One last thing," said Cherry. "You've worked right round Mars shell, Chi. Can you read this for me?" He handed Nailer the card which had been left by his mysterious visitor.

The circus-marshal took the card, scanned it, and went stiff.

"Where the hell did you get this?"

"A character who was in here earlier, half man, half can. Reckons he's going to have a proposition for me."

"You entertain a proposition from Land-a?" Nailer's voice trailed into incredulity. "Cherry, you twisted old nut, you're becoming the victim of your own illusions."

"Why? Who is he?"

"He's a notorious prince from Hammanite, one of the farside regions outside the Federation. For some reason, when his part of the shell was being terraformed, all the platinum in the total specification got dumped in one spot—a whole mountain range of it. He's reckoned to be the richest man on Mars shell."

"So why does that upset you?"

"Because he uses his money to buy people. He imagines himself a sort of super-scientist, always arranging strange experiments and expeditions."

"That doesn't sound too bad to me."

"Cherry—most of the people he hires are never seen again. Better you go down with a fatal disease than get involved with Land-a. Tell you what I'll do for you. I'll have Circus Admin replace your bubble-hall free of charge. After all, it was their mains which blew it."

"In return for what?" asked Cherry guardedly.

"Forget about Land-a. And if he comes back with a proposition, don't even consider it. You may be the bane of my life, but I wouldn't wish a fate like that on you. Believe me, Cherry, I've been all round Mars shell. I know what I'm talking about." He stopped to answer the communicator on his belt, then sucked his lip. "There's a police hunter-killer squad asking permission to land on our pads. I wonder which of you brigands they're after this time?"

Tez, his head bandaged and his face cleansed of blood, came back to the illusionist just as the disaster team pulled out.

"What are you going to do about Castor, Cherry? Chi isn't fooling when he says he'll have you out of the circus if he catches you having another crack at him."

"My boy," said Cherry amiably, "perhaps we needn't worry too much about Chi. How would you like to work in a proper holo-establishment—everything fixed and permanent and computerised? How about our own holo-theatre?"

"Sounds like heaven, Cherry. Did you get a crack on the head too?"

"No. But I think I've got a patron—a big one. Somebody so powerful he even scares the pants off Chi Nailer."

"And he'd back us?"

"I think he might. He owns a whole mountain of platinum. Chi's warned me off, but I think it's only jealousy. If it's the last thing I do in circus, I'm going to have one last crack at Castor. If Chi gets unreasonable about it, then we've still this other possibility left to fall back on. Go get your scratchpad, Tez, and let's get down to some planning. This has to be a real masterpiece of holo-illusion—just in case it should also be our farewell performance.

CHAPTER THREE

Enter Mistress Sin

IN THE earlier days of the frantic race to construct more living space for a human population growing nearly exponentially, absolute control by Zeus had not yet been established. At that time, the first great shell of the Solarian system was starting to be built around the twenty-four terraformed worlds of Mars-orbit, and thirty-one new worlds were being constructed in the

Asteroid belt. Yet despite these mind-staggering increases in available living space, the old lessons in the history of over-population had bitten deeply, and much unauthorised emigration took place even to new-made worlds not yet finished for human habitation.

Some of these earlier "pirate" colonies became cut off from all contact with main-stream humanity for many centuries, and their loss and eventual rediscovery gave rise to many legends. One of the more curious of these tales concerns a dissident political community which settled a new-made world in Mars-orbit, called Engel. Their communal policy of absolute equality for all living things blasted their society apart when they found themselves co-sharing the planet, so it is said, with some curi-ously aquatic creatures who were fully gene-compatible.

Critics of the story can produce abundant proof that such a happening was a biological and evolutionary impossibility. What-ever the origin of the mutant strain, however, the results are consistent with the fact that a mere four generations of cohabita-tion so hopelessly entangled the bloodlines that the resultant hybrids had to be accepted as a new ethnic group. Their skins were tinged with green, their aquatic abilities were astonishing, and their rapacity, guile and lack of conscience became legends in themselves.

The final construction of the Mars shell and the relegation of Engel to the status of a "caged" world spread the wily green Engelians far and wide. As is often the case with descendants of unrelated gene-stock, many bore the dominant traits of both parental bloodlines. The men were frequently handsome and athletic, whilst most of the women were possessed of an outlandish, heart-stopping attractiveness which made them virtually impossi-ble either to ignore or forget. Both sexes were characterised by a keen intelligence, and all shared the common traits of acquisitive-ness and lack of conscience. And one of the more attractive of these deadly daughters was Sine Anura.

The relevance of this digression is that not more than a mile from the scene of Cherry's recent misfortune, on one of the minor ways where circus rents were cheap and the side-shows made little pretence at finesse, there was a hard-topped hall devoted to exploiting the talents of one, Mistress Sin, "The Sea Devil's Daughter", who, unexpectedly if her claimed parentage was true, had to fight naked under water three times daily with loathsome and dangerous sea creatures in order to make a living.

That Sine Anura and Mistress Sin were one and the same is obvious. What was not obvious was the fact that the sea creatures she fought were perfectly genuine and fully as dangerous as the signs proclaimed, and that the elements of showmanship were here truthfully surpassed by the truly amazing aquatic and combatant abilities of Mistress Sin herself.

A further fact which was concealed was that Sine Anura was wanted by the Federation police on no less than sixteen counts, and that she had chosen to run with the Solarian Circus as a way of achieving anonymity without limiting her freedom to travel, because her major talents were other than those she displayed on the creatures in the tank.

It was directly to this unlikely venue that the silently-wheeled Land-a and his retinue proceeded. Their choice of destination was obviously no casual affair, and their arrival in the closed period between shows was no accident of timing. Treem Admel, Mistress Sin's manager, and a man seemingly on the very edge of physical and mental collapse, was on a high stage effecting the transfer of some particularly dangerous sea creatures from security containers into the demonstration tank when one of Land-a's aides smashed down the flimsy door of the hall. The shock of the surprise entry was such that the pallid and shaking Treem nearly leaped into the tank himself, a situation he would have had no capacity to survive.

"We're closed—go away! The next showing is at twenty-seven hours."

Land-a's silent wheels bore him into the auditorium, and his team became neatly deployed around him. He looked at the wan and shaking Treem, and his expression was one of extreme disgust.

"Where's the hell-bitch Sine Anura?"

Treem's mouth was wide with fear and fascination. He had never before considered anything as daunting as a man with only head and arms, and with the rest of what was left of him completely enclosed in a wheeled container. He struggled to become articulate again.

"Do you mean Mistress Sin?"

"I mean Sine Anura—whatever alias she's adopting this year. Fetch her, or I'll have you fed to those filthy fish, and do the job myself."

The luckless Treem stole one despairing glance at the horrific occupants of the demonstration tank and descended hastily from the high staging.

"I'll try to wake her, but she's resting. She'll be very angry. Who shall I say wants her?"

At a nod from Land-a, one of the aides handed him a card imprinted with silver hieroglyphics.

"Give her that. She'll understand."

"What will I understand?" Sine had quietly come in from behind them. Taken by surprise, the whole group turned about to face the green-tinged hostility of the incredibly attractive girl who had them all covered by a broad-beamed photon gun.

Land-a nodded to an aide to offer her a card. She made no attempt to take it, and indicated that the fellow should keep his distance, though her sharp eyes focused narrowly on the silver legend.

"The writing I don't read," she said. "But the smell I recognise. Prince Land-a, who imagines he owns everyone on Mars shell."

"At your service!" said Land-a evenly.

"You're way out of your territory, Land-a. What sort of carrion hunt fetches you this far into civilisation?"

"Carrion like Sine Anura, I ask you to believe. I'm recruiting skills for one of my little projects, and it's surprising what wild and deadly talents one finds in the shades of the Solarian Circus."

"Why call on me? There are . . . others."

"Few as totally lacking in conscience or as practiced in lies. None I think as skilled in seduction and erotica."

"You're wasting your time, Land-a. I'm not interested in your schemes."

"You've forgotten my reputation. I always get what I want. I've even taken out insurance on the outcome. The Federation police have been informed of who and where you are. My information is that a hunter-killer squad is already on its way."

"You work with the hunters?" For the first time the girl's certainty seemed to crack.

"A purely circumstantial arrangement," said Land-a smoothly. "And the circumstance is that I have the only ship on this part of the shell which the police can't touch. Not only do I have diplomatic immunity, but I can out-talk, outrun and outshoot anything this forsaken sector of Mars shell has to offer. Your choice is simple—you know what the psyches will do to you if they ever get you pinned down in a police cell. Why take the risk, Mistress Sin. I'm here to offer you my protection in return for a few favours."

For one moment Sine Anura allowed her attention to waver. As the photon gun in her hand drifted from its deadly focus, so one of Land-a's henchmen launched himself like a tiger in an attempt to smash the weapon from her hands. Land-a gave a little involuntary cry of alarm at the projected outcome of such an ill-advised assault.

Sine Anura sidestepped easily and allowed the gun to be knocked away. Unthinkingly the fellow followed the gun, but as he passed Anura her delicate green fingers merely brushed each side of his neck just below the ears. Stunned by some bolt of energy he had no reason to anticipate, the fellow screamed and was suddenly silent as he was literally flung upwards by the violent spasm of his own muscles. His trajectory rammed his head against the security rim of the demonstration tank, and he slumped to the floor like a broken doll, whilst dangerous and loathsome sea creatures looked out, full of curiosity and hunger.

By this time another of Land-a's aides was covering the girl with his own weapon, whilst the prince swiftly appraised the condition of his fallen protector.

"He's dead, you hell-bitch! I ought to kill you for that."

"But you won't. You'd not be here in person unless I was valuable to you. All right, Land-a! You've made your point. Now let's get out of here before the police arrive." She turned and looked at the body of the fallen bodyguard. "What do you want to do with him?"

Land-a regarded the body of his fallen comrade with something akin to regret, then suddenly came to the point of decision. "We can't carry him out without attracting attention, so we'd better feed him to the fish. I always suspected you had an electro-muscular system, but I hadn't anticipated it was quite so deadly."

"You've not seen its limits yet," said Anura savagely. "I could drop the rest of you without having to think about it. Remember that, if any of you get any strange ideas about our relationship."

Her gaze suddenly fell on the frightened form of Treem Admel, who was cowering beneath the steps leading to the high staging.

"Come out, Weasel! I don't like witnesses. It's untidy."

Treem emerged with the greatest reluctance, his face literally writhing with nervous tension.

"I saw nothing, honestly! I swear they'll never make me speak."

Sine Anura moved deliberately towards him, and the hapless Treem watched her approach with a degree of fear that bordered on hypnotic fascination, his eyes never once ceasing to watch her delicate green fingers. Then at the very last instant before she touched him he shot one last glance of agonised appeal towards Land-a. Sine's fingers touched the fellow's bare arms, merely caressing the flesh. She was playing with him, both of them knowing he was within a second of death, while she sadistically enjoyed the sensation of her power over him.

"Leave him!" said Land-a suddenly. "He can do us no harm, and one death already is sufficient. Let's get clear of here before the hunter-killers arrive."

Reluctantly Sine Anura let her victim go, shocking him just enough to make him spin back with a cry. Then he collapsed shivering at the feet of his terrible mistress. She rolled him over disdainfully with her foot.

"If you ever speak about this day to anyone, I'll come back and finish what I started."

Land-a instructed his aides to remove the body of their former comrade from the floor to the tank, and watched in silent speculation as the sea creatures moved in for the feast. It was not lost on him that this fearsome tank was also the place where Sine Anura sported herself thrice daily to amuse a gaping crowd. This confirmed what his researches had already told him: that Sine Anura well deserved her reputation for being one of the cleverest and most dangerous women in creation.

At the edge of the circus landing pads, Maq Ancor watched the arrival of the sinister darts of the Federation hunter-killer squads with wary interest. Withdrawal of the shadowy political support which gave registered guild assassins relative immunity from police interference, had left him uncomfortably exposed. His folio of past triumphs in the deadly arts was now police property, and there were no restraints inhibiting his arrest and trial for half a hundred executions now renamed murders.

In ordinary circumstances, Maq was afraid of no man. His professional training and abilities, plus the specialised weapons he had managed to retain, made him more than a match for any ten ordinary armed policemen. The black-tunicked men of the hunter-killer squads, however, were a different proposition. They moved on in highly-trained trios, were equipped with weapons and shields not available from any common weaponmaster, and had skills in detention and death dealing which even a professional assassin might envy. The odds were millions to one against his being the target of this particular swoop, yet the timing and coincidence of place held his gut with uncomfortable fingers.

The police squads were met on the field by the circus-marshal, who led them swiftly away down an adjoining promenade. This gave Ancor a shaft of hope. The speed of their departure betrayed a certainty of their destination, and their heading was towards part of the circus where he had not yet strayed.

The ex-assassin relaxed, and renewed his survey of the ships on the pads, attempting to guess the identity of his unknown patron. Having investigated types of residence available to the supremely rich in the vicinity of the circus, he had become convinced that his mysterious benefactor could only be one of those owning a private exospheric ship. His favourite choice was a tall, utilitarian vessel with a drive complex which suggested it must have been close to the most powerful thing in Aster-space. The identification legends were in characters he did not begin to understand: but it was the lithe watchfulness of its armed hatch-guard which attracted his attention. These were not casual ratings, but men whose training had obviously been supervised by a master with more than average acumen.

Ancor retired to the wide grassy strip at the edge of the field and lay down and feigned sleep, his head covered with a coloured kerchief. Through the bright, reflexive cloth he was able to keep watch on the vessel, hopefully without any observers aboard being able to detect his detailed interest. His surveillance told him little he had not already established, but he was interested when a remarkably attractive green-skinned girl was ushered in through the hatch. Her glance towards the ship-mass before she entered suggested that this was the first time she had ever boarded the vessel, and he mentally marked her as probably a hired concubine being brought to amuse the owner of the ship.

Even while being immersed in these speculations, Ancor had not forgotten the assassins' cardinal principle of guarding his own back. The detector on his wrist, sensitive to any change in the steady-state of his local environment, gave him ample warning of a wheeled stranger's approach. Without even appearing to move, Ancor brought his own weapon to bear beneath his cloak, and could have dropped the intruder at any time he chose. Photon gun in hand, the stranger headed straight for Ancor, and the assassin had to repress a slight smile at the naivety of this approach.

The silent wheels drew close and halted.

"Move one muscle," said Ancor quietly through the cloth, "and you're a dead man."

A dark brow darkened further. "I think the advantage is already mine." The bright sky behind the man's head made it difficult to discern the features, but power and intellect were written into the brow and jawline. "Who are you? And why do you spy on my ship?"

"I was watching and wondering."

"Wondering what?"

"Why a man who already possesses so many formidable employees should think it worth paying so much to hire yet another."

The wheeled man relaxed. "Ah, Assassin Ancor, I believe! I was expecting you. But it hardly pleases me to be able to take a trained assassin with my own hands."

"You've taken nothing. Your life has been balanced on a knife edge since the moment you came into sight. Your photon gun won't work, because I've a neutralising field in operation."

As proof of this Ancor reached up and without diverting the gun from his temple, he forced the holder to squeeze the trigger. Nothing happened, and the scowling stranger examined the gun disgustedly before throwing it savagely away.

"My apologies, Assassin Ancor! Every man to his trade. I should have known better than to tangle with an expert. Come into the ship. We've a great deal to discuss. And I think one of your future comrades will need a little of our encouragement to bring him quietly into the fold."

CHAPTER FOUR

Expatriation

CHI NAILER was roused by a persistent sound which penetrated the walls of his high office overlooking the circus. He swiftly identified it as the engine note of a stratospheric craft in trouble. Through his binoculars, he saw one of the circus's own bulk supply freighters trembling on erratic downthrust jets and obviously unable to gain sufficient steerage to take it safely over the landing pads.

Nailer hit the controls of his communications set and was instantly in contact with his own disaster-control centre.

"What's the status of that freighter in trouble over zone five?"

"You reckon it's a freighter, Chi? Our radar says it's a lot smaller."

"We'll all be a lot smaller if it falls slap into the middle of the circus," said Nailer irritably. "If that ship comes down, where's it liable to hit?"

"Fairly central in zone five. Say around Harry Castor's pitch."

"Right! I want zone five evacuated, and the whole area to go under circus-law until I say the emergency is over."

"Understood, Chi. Emergency procedures starting now. What's the other big exercise this evening?"

"None that I know of. Why?"

"The power generation manager is complaining of not having been notified of undue load. Somebody is already taking the average twilight load for the entire circus—and we've not even started lighting-up yet."

"Get him to trace where the bulk of that power is going. Then have Security pick up Cherry and sit on him until I can arrange his cremation—live."

"Hell! You can't have Cherry arrested just for using power. He could be using it legitimately."

"Birth included, nothing about that old bastard has ever been legitimate."

"You're not suggesting that crashing 'strato is a terrain hologram? There's definitely something up there, Chi. We've got it clear on our screens."

"I don't know what the hell I'm suggesting. But the fact the thing appears to be crashing on Harry Castor is a mighty strange coincidence."

Near the centre of zone five Nailer drove up the prepared ramp to the local disaster-control point. The stricken craft had now halved its height since first sighting, and was carpeting the whole area with an erratic pattern of engine sounds which grew more daunting by the second. Swift appraisal told Nailer that it was indeed a circus freighter, and moreover one of those engaged in the bulk transport of oils and flammable liquids.

Few of the onlookers were convinced that the ship would actually fall, and nearly all felt that even if it did, they themselves were already safely removed from the point of impact. Knowing the nature of the cargo, Nailer was forced to disagree, and called on extra security men to speed the clearance of the area. Amongst the circus operators there was an even greater reluctance to leave, for fear of looting of their establishments in their absence. In particular, one Harry Castor chained himself to a door handle of his exhibition hall and swallowed the key.

With the stalling stratocraft only seconds from its final dive, Nailer raced up with cutters, severed the chain, and rendered Harry Castor unconscious with a single punch which followed through to become a fireman's lift. Driven by one of his own disaster team, his own vehicle whirled down the ramp to meet him, and literally throwing the unconscious Castor into the back, Nailer hung on to the exterior projections as the vehicle rocketed away from the scene. Seconds later the freighter fell with an impact which shook the ground, and then exploded with a truly frightening fire-ball which fully confirmed Nailer's worst misgivings.

At a reasonable distance Nailer ordered the vehicle to a halt, and climbed on to the roof, the better to estimate how far the leaping tongues of flaming oil were likely to spread. At a rough guess they would be lucky to confine the multiple fires merely within zone five.

A shout from his driver caused him to look down. Harry Castor had awoken, and was running back towards the flames, shrieking something incoherent at the top of his ragged voice. Nailer leaped from the vehicle roof and brought him down with a flying tackle.

"What's got into you, you crazy old fox?" he asked.

"Me crazy? You're the one who's crazy!" Castor was literally weeping with emotion. "You're letting him get away with it!"

"Letting who get away with what?"

"Cherry, of course, the old faker!"

"Are you trying to tell me all that is a terrain hologram?"

"Of course it is, you idiot! Can't you see the fringes where their projectors don't balance? Did you ever *really* see flames that colour? Oh God! Why must I always be surrounded by fools?"

Castor, however, had finished up talking to himself. Nailer had hurtled along the promenade to where the nearest flames licked hungrily at the painted wall. It took him less than a second to decide that the paint was untouched by fire and that the tongues of flame were only a cold illusion. Then swearing and cursing like one demented, the circus-marshal headed back to the radio in his vehicle.

"Disaster-centre, get this! Cut all electrical power to zone five and chop every source Cherry might have been using."

"Order being executed, Chi. What's the problem?"

"That crash was one of Cherry's bloody holo-tricks."

"But it wasn't, Chi. There was a craft went down. We tracked it. Like I said, not a freighter—something smaller."

"Get the power off," said Nailer wearily. "And get me Cherry. I'll get to the bottom of this . . . preferably over his dead body."

As the circuits were disconnected, much that had seemed irrevocably destroyed was found to be undamaged. As he superintended this strange restoration, however, Nailer began to be aware of a real source of heat. It was finally established that under cover of the illusion a pilotless strato-drone had indeed fallen out of the air and exploded in the centre of Castor's establishment. The damage to the property was considerable, but fortunately nothing like as widespread as the original illusion had made it appear.

Whilst Nailer was waiting for the fire-crews, a commotion at the far side caught his attention. He went round and found Cherry, dressed as ever in a plain white toga, and obviously very drunk, attempting to resist his arrest by the security corpsmen. As Nailer advanced, Cherry tore his arms free from his captors and held his hands towards the heavens in what he hoped was a commanding gesture.

"I, Cherry, bring you illusions more real than reality it-self . . ."

"And I, Chi Nailer, will bring you punishments more lingering than purgatory," said Nailer.

"Not so! I've resigned from the circus, Chi. You can't touch me."

"Oh, I can touch you all right, Cherry! There's about five million credits to pay for the damage just to this little lot, without mentioning the compensation the circus will want."

Cherry swayed drunkenly. Then, incredibly, he turned and tried to walk straight into the living fire, apparently convinced that the bright flames were part of his own holo-illusion. He must have taken a dozen steps before the reality of the smoke and the heat dawned upon his befuddled senses, and he returned at a funny little gallop, his toga smouldering, his face ashen, and his mind suddenly cleared.

"I didn't do this, Chi! Honest to God, I didn't! All I did was to create an illusion. So where did the ship come from? This fire? Believe me, Chi! Believe me!"

Nailer turned to the security corps-men. "Take this idiot to my office and sober him up. There's a lot of questions I want answered before we hand him over to the police. And pick up his two assistants, Tez and Carli. Cherry's too damn lazy to have engineered this whole thing on his own."

When the field was safe, Nailer sent in his experts to search for pieces of the sky-drone which had caused the actual damage, hoping that it would be possible to identify the person responsible for its despatch. Cherry was a megalomaniac and a born prankster, but he was insufficiently vicious to reinforce one of his own illusions with a crashing 'drone. For some reason, Cherry was being used.

Most of the emergency had been righted when Chi Nailer received a call from his own office.

"Problems here, Chi. Man from the provost's office, and another character, with a writ of habeas corpus for Cherry and his two assistants."

"Well, they can't have them. I've not finished with them yet."

"Then you'd better get over here, Chi. Because I can't stop them."

As Nailer stormed up the office steps he was confronted by a sheepishly triumphant Cherry, a nervous and white-faced Tez, and an extremely angry Carli. What made Nailer swear, however, was the sight of Land-a, smug and serene in his body carriage. The civilian from the provost's office was polite but firm. The three individuals in Nailer's custody, he said, were legal citizens of the independent Mars-shell State of Hammanite, which did not recognise the Federation's right to restrain her subjects.

"Hammanite rubbish!" shouted Nailer. "Cherry's been with the circus since he was a tadpole. He's never been to the Hammanite States in his life."

"Perhaps I should explain." Land-a moved forward on silent wheels. "My ship is legally Hammanite territory, and these three have recently joined my staff. All have accepted Hammanite citizenship, and are now covered by the diplomatic immunity which is our right."

Nailer spat in disgust. "I heard you were out collecting garbage, Land-a. But you've certainly made a mistake this time. Cherry's no asset. He's a positive liability. Always has been. Always will be."

"Magician Cherry has talents I shall find very useful."

"Cherry!" said Nailer despairingly. "You don't know what the hell you're getting into. Get out of it now, while you still can."

"I've resigned from the circus," said Cherry stoutly. "After all these years my talents have been recognised."

"Look, you twisted old nut, if I agree to bring no charges against you for today's episode, will you stay?"

"Sorry, Chi! Great talent must have its outlet."

"I hope for your sake you still feel that way when you wake with a hangover in the morning." He turned to Tez and Carli, but the man from the provost's office intervened.

"You've had your say, Nailer, and you've produced no

reason to show why these farside citizens shouldn't be allowed to return to their lawful territory. Attempt any further hindrance and you'll render yourself liable to action for interference with due legal rights.''

"Legal!" shouted Nailer. "What's legal about all this? These three have been tricked into adopting Hammanite citizenship by manipulating them into trouble with the Federation police. That's both coercion and abduction, and you stand there and talk about legality.''

"I recommend you guard your tongue more carefully, Nailer, lest you leave yourself open to further charges.''

"Get out of here the lot of you!" said Nailer tiredly. "Suddenly I see the justice of it all—a sort of poetical justice. Cherry hanged by his own ego, and Land-a, of all people taking over my yoke and my cross. Very funny . . . when you look at it in the right way. By the way, Land-a, if you want back the bits of your sky-drone, you can collect them any time. I would sure hate to be arrested for the felonious retention of your personal property.''

CHAPTER FIVE

Search for the Sun!

ABOARD THE exospheric ship, in a stateroom of great opulence, Cherry, Sine Anura and Maq Ancor sat around a circular table of solid burnished platinum inset into which concentric bands of gold studded with precious stones represented the stylised picture of the Solarian universe. At the centrepoint of the display, however, where Cherry's imagery had depicted the popular concept of a great black singularity, there here resided one immense and marvellous ruby which, a tribute to the lapidary's art, shone more splendidly than any other item in the room. Responding to some empathic feed-back from his brain, Land-a's life-support carriage rode slowly back and forth at the table's edge as an indication of his impatience to begin, but his voice and manner were the surest indication of his mastery.

"You are naturally wondering why I went to such great lengths to gather the three of you together. The answer is simple: I've a job to be done which requires a special blend of skills and talents. I've researched many years to find the best possible combination of these, and spent several further years locating the best practitioners. You are my chosen team, each selected from a thousand possible alternatives. To ensure your co-operation, you will each of you be rewarded more handsomely than you could have imagined. I would furthermore remind you that all of you are wanted in some degree by the Federation police, and that your best defence against them is to remain in my employment."

"I didn't put that drone down there," said Cherry unhappily.

"You created your climactic masterpiece as a grand finale to your career in the circus, Magician Cherry. Admittedly it was reinforced by us with a little solid realism, but the talent to create illusions more real than reality has untold potential when a different reality is concealed beneath. You will see."

He turned to Sine Anura, who had been studying her new master with a green and slightly mocking smile, though her gaze wandered occasionally to the strong, engaging ugliness of the Lion's face.

"And now to Mistress Sin. Her talents are equally unique. Her specialities are seduction and erotica, which have powers in certain human situations where even force of arms might fail. However, lest anyone should be tempted to jump into bed with her, they should be warned that she also has an electro-muscular system donated by her fishy ancestry. This enables her fingers to deliver discharges up to six thousand volts. Despite her attractions, or perhaps because of them, Mistress Sin is a very deadly lady."

Mischievously, Sine Anura placed a casual hand on the platinum table. Land-a saw the movement and withdrew his fingers sharply from contact with the metal: Ancor, his hands habitually within unimpeded range of his weapons, was similarly out of contact: and it was Cherry who leaped to his feet with an aggrieved shout as Sine's playful charge shocked his resting arm.

Land-a treated her to a deep scowl, then turned his attention to Maq.

"And what do I say about you, Assassin Ancor? You're a skilled killer, dangerous, desperate and hunted. An angry human wasp. You shall be the leader of our team. I think you'll not find your talents under-used."

Ancor looked up. "You haven't yet told us what job this is which requires so much of its participants."

"I was about to, Assassin Ancor. But before we get to detail, let us talk about the Solarian universe."

Land-a turned on silent wheels, and although confined to his grotesque life-supporting carriage he achieved the impression of drawing himself up and towering above them, fixing them with a gaze nearly hypnotic in its intensity.

"One of the most fantastic things about Solaria is how little we really know about it. We ourselves were born beneath a region called Aster-space, which is simply that area of space between the concentric shells of Mars-orbit and Asteroid-orbit. We think we know—because the books tell us—that there are smaller shells inside the Mars shell, and greater ones outside the Asteroid shell. What is difficult to accept is that that bare statement is all that anyone on Mars shell actually knows about Solaria. Is it infinite or is it finite? What lies inside it, and what lies outside? Shockingly, none of us knows."

He paused as if expecting a protest, but none came. Cherry was examining his shocked arm, Maq Ancor was listening intently but not dissenting, and Sine Anura was contemplating Ancor's lion-like head with something akin to admiration. Land-a continued.

"I think the best way we can understand Solaria is to look at it historically. The earliest records I can find invariably speak of 'the world' as though there was only one in the beginning. One world and a sun. Soon afterwards there's a reference to the 'sixteen worlds in Terran-orbit' and the word terraforming regularly appears in the texts. There is also the first mention of Zeus as 'the fantastic cybernetic device which superintends the gravitational seeding of the dust and gas clouds in space and brings back aggregates unimaginably large from regions where no man could possibly go.'

"I think we can safely assume the original world had, as we have ourselves, a population growing at a roughly exponential rate. Somehow they managed to make themselves a second world, then soon had to double-up and double again, until they had sixteen worlds in the same orbit. The next reference we can find speaks of 'eleven worlds in Venus-orbit and twenty-four in Mars.' The interesting thing about all this is that in the early days there appears to have been a partnership between the human constructors and Zeus. Man had not yet abandoned his destiny entirely to the machine, and Zeus was then a space-construction complex rather than the overall arbiter of all our destinies, as it is today."

"Have you any idea when that first relationship with Zeus broke down?" asked Ancor.

"No. But I think it has something to do with the creation of the shells. Given access to the unlimited material, which Zeus appears to have been able to harvest from the clouds in space, filling the entire orbital diameter with a vast spherical shell instead of a handful of scattered worlds obviously provided a fantastic increase in available living space. As far as we know, the Mars shell was the first to be constructed, and it is that which seems to have marked the turning point in the relationship between Zeus and man. You see, the tubular highways through the thickness of the shell, which are the focal points of the spoke-shuttle system, work one way only—from inside to outside. They can not be reversed.

"Since the building of the Mars shell, we in Aster-space have been completely dependent on Zeus for the energy supply to fuel our luminaries, and completely cut off from any information about what lies within the shell. Then the thirty-nine worlds of Asteroid-orbit were incorporated in the Asteroid shell, and Aster-space was effectively sealed off from the rest of the Solarian universe. Now we cannot know the truth of what lies within Mars-orbit. Nor may we ever know what lies outside the Asteroid shell unless Zeus directs us to emigrate—in which case we cannot return to tell what we know."

Cherry was growing a little perplexed.

"But of course we know about the inner-shells. We have books, pictures . . ."

"All of which were brought out by our ancestors when Mars shell was first being populated. None of the old records have been updated since, and fully half of them are as liable to be fiction as fact. Too many legends, Magician Cherry, and no way of discerning which is closest to reality."

"Can't we ask Zeus?" asked Sine Anura. "If it built the Solarian universe it must surely know what it has made."

"I think to answer that, Mistress Sin, we must again examine history," said Land-a. "If the density of an expanding population is to be controlled by emigration, the policy must be rigidly enforced. I gather that the earlier human-controlled population schemes were notorious for their graft and corruption. It made sense to let Zeus, who already did the head-count via the Solarian Identifile, also police the system. Zeus alone could not be bribed."

"So?"

"This in turn generated a new problem. If Zeus couldn't be bribed, it might still be possible to destroy it or render it less effective, and there are many accounts of this being attempted. But as far as we know, Zeus' ancient programers built into it two prime directives. The first is that it shall continue to construct sufficient living space for the ever-increasing race of man. The second, that it should permit no actual or potential interference with the attainment of the first directive.

"The second directive is our stumbling point. Since to attack a machine one needs to know something about it and the environment in which it functions, Zeus interprets any interrogation about itself or the structure of the Solarian universe as the possible prelude to an attack. Such an attitude in a human being would be called paranoia, but in a machine it's a logical and proven factor for enabling it to follow its first directive. My researches prove that asking questions about Solaria is a hundred per cent lethal.''

"You're very positive about the figure," said Sine Anura critically.

"Indeed, yes. I've hired many people to try it. Not one of them survived Zeus' manseekers.''

"So what do you expect of us?" asked Ancor.

"For you, the culmination of all my research and all my years of planning. I want you to make an expedition right through to the centre of Solaria. I want you to see and record every detail, and sort out the fact from the fiction. I want you to go and search for the sun which breathed life into human kind. It's a project I've dreamt of for a lifetime, but being confined in this abominable apparatus, I would be unable to stand the stresses of such a journey. Therefore you will be my eyes and my ears, ask my questions, and retail my sense of wonder.''

He was speaking now to Ancor alone. The two men seemed to have established a degree of rapport which went deeply beyond the actual words. Sine Anura and Cherry both waited to hear the results of Ancor's deep consideration. Finally Maq said: "Seeing that you've already explained that such a journey is impossible, how do you propose we might bring it about?''

"In this way, Assassin Ancor. I mentioned just now that each orbit first had a number of individual worlds, before these were incorporated into a shell. These worlds were not destroyed, but, with orbits carefully realigned, were left spinning in their places, rather like ball-bearings in a 'cage'.''

"The cageworlds. What of them?''

"My researches suggest that the interspace between the cageworlds and the thickness of the shells in which they reside may form a potential route through to the other side of the shell and hence to the space beyond.''

"I've heard it said that such a journey is impossible.''

"It *was* impossible, Assassin Ancor. There were no craft which could withstand the conditions of vacuum, pressure and turbulence in the interspace. But over many years I've had such a craft developed. It has the requisite toughness and durability to take it through what we know of interspace conditions. It has

true space-going potential and the power resources to take it
through to the centre of Solaria and back again. And it has
atmospheric-flight capabilities which can permit it to fly, hover,
or to land without a prepared site. Never before did such a craft
exist.''

"Does it also have armaments?'' asked Ancor.

"Enough to fight a minor war—if that satisfies you, Assassin.''

"Barely. If I read this correctly, human and environmental
hazards will be the least of our worries. If Zeus is paranoid about
the mere asking of questions, how much more is it going to react
against an actual expedition?''

"The answer is that you'll be up against the force which was
powerful enough to build the Solarian universe. A challenge of
that order is why I need a man like you to lead my expedition.
And I'll tell you why I call it a challenge rather than a threat.
While you're through to the inner shells I want you to seek out
the nucleus of Zeus itself and see if the old relationship between
man and Zeus can possibly be re-established. What do you say,
Assassin Ancor?''

"I think,'' said the Lion, "that if there was one reason could
tempt me to go along with this insane venture, it would be the
chance to re-open that dialogue. I'm your man, Land-a.''

Finally the meeting ended, and Land-a dismissed a frightened
and downcast Cherry and a pensive Mistress Sin. As Ancor
turned to go, however, the wheeled man called him back.

"A private word, Assassin Ancor. You will know me by now
for the thoroughness of my researches. For instance, I know
more about you than do your family and all your friends put
together. There were two questions about you to which I could
find no answer. Firstly, why one of your background and aca-
demic standing should become an assassin in the first place?
Secondly, when you were unfrocked, why did the guild react
against you as violently as they did?''

"Your researches,'' said the Lion enigmatically, "can reveal
only facts which have been established. One can only guess at
human motivation.''

CHAPTER SIX

Strange companions

"LOOK, CARLI," said Tez finally, "it's no use keeping on at me. I didn't exactly aim for us to become Hammanite citizens. But it's probably better than ten years in a police pen."

Carli refused to be mollified. "If you hadn't helped that crackpot Cherry with his idiot scheme, we wouldn't be in trouble with the police in the first place."

"We've been through all this a hundred times," said Tez wearily. "Cherry's the boss, right? He owns the show and pays the wages. When he wants a terrain hologram, I produce it. What else should I do? Spit in his face?"

"What makes you think Cherry is actually going to build this wretched holo-theatre?"

"He's shown me the money, Carli. Sufficient for the whole damn works."

"Fat lot of good that'll do us now we've given up Federation citizenship!"

"There must be plenty of territories outside the Federation."

"Which have holo shows? They're all populated by fat, greasy little men gloating over their harems. Sex is all they want— solid, not holo."

"Well, you're not in a harem yet." Tez was beginning to lose his patience. "We'll see what Cherry says when he gets back."

"The old crow is senile and demented. He thinks all life is a holo show—that you can walk out when you get tired of it. Well this time the crazy old fool has got us into something which won't go away when they cut the power."

She turned over and lay face down, sobbing into the silken pillow. Tez tried to comfort her, but she warded him off with a backhand gesture which unfortunately caught him on the end of the nose. Sulkily he returned to the outer cabin to await the illusionist's return.

To complete Tez's misery and apprehension, the ship made a perfectly controlled take-off while he sat, and on powerful motors clawed its way into the exosphere, its engine song fading plaintively as it achieved the vast silences of Aster-space. Then

Cherry came back and offered Tez a small, golden, pressurised
vial.

"A present from Land-a for you and Carli."

"What do we do with it, drink it?"

"No, you spray it on her. Makes her soft, warm and responsive.
Hammanites use it in their harems. Results guaranteed."

Tez pocketed the vial. "The mood she's in right now, I guess
I'd need about a gallon. Are we going to get the holo-theatre,
Cherry?"

The illusionist sat down. He looked older and more frail and
skeletal than Tez ever remembered noticing before.

"Later, Tez. I've got the money, but first we have to earn it.
We've a job to do."

"What sort of job, Cherry?" Carli had left her bed and was
standing in the doorway. Her voice was sheer acid.

Cherry started to hedge, then saw the look in Carli's eyes and
decided to get the truth over quickly.

"We're going on an expedition. I want Tez along to help with
the equipment. And you can come—" he searched his mind for
some task he could usefully assign to her "—and do the cooking."

"Cooking!" Her outrage was nearly complete. "And where's
this expedition to, Cherry, you daft old buzzard?"

"Right through to the centre of Solaria," said Cherry, searching for a bottle.

Meanwhile, in his own suite, Maq Ancor opened the door in
response to a quiet knock, and the attractive Sine Anura slipped
in. He holstered his weapon reluctantly, and offered her a couch.

"Have you any idea what we've got ourselves into, Maq?"
she asked seriously.

"Just a little." He was studying the excellence of her pose
and the casual artistry of her manner. Through her heady perfume his keen nose detected just a hint of sex-attractant pheromone.

"This whole thing is insane," she said. "Why choose such an
unlikely trio as us to form an expedition?"

"I've been wondering the same thing myself. As I read it,
Land-a has tried this exercise before—possibly many times. He's
analysed his failures and come up with a combination so improba-
ble that it couldn't have been deduced from first principles. It
has to be a formula which has evolved through trial and error."

"And what if we're to be another unsuccessful trial?"

"Then I presume he modifies the equation and starts again."

"That wasn't quite what I meant. I want to get off, Maq. That
bastard engineered me into taking this trip, and I don't owe him

any favours. I understand we're putting down at Zin-Zan for supplies. What about us making a break together?''

"There's no way!" said Ancor evenly. "Unfrocked I may be, but I'm still an assassin by profession. I've taken his money, therefore I'm his till the contract ends. Apart from which, I see the expedition as a pleasanter prospect than being hounded around the Mars shell territories until the day I make my last mistake. I would have thought the same applied to you.''

"Well, if you won't come, at least help me to get away. I rate my chances of staying alive in the Federation higher than if I continue with Land-a's mad obsession.''

Ancor poured a drink and offered it to her, carefully avoiding contact with her fingers.

"Don't you think Land-a realises all this? In Zin-Zan you'll be guarded like the Hammanite crown jewels. You'll have no opportunity for escape. The time to make a break is when it's least expected, not when it's most anticipated.''

"And that's your professional advice? Play for later?"

"No, that's merely common sense. My professional advice is not to discuss double-crossing a person like Land-a in a room he's had ample opportunity to bug.''

She looked up sharply. "Is it bugged?"

"It was, but I found and deactivated them earlier. No assassin could be expected to do less.''

"Why should he bother to bug your cabin?"

Ancor laughed. "Because he seems to have some idea that I'm something more than I claim to be.''

"Are you sure you got them all?"

"Certainly I'm sure. Had I not, Land-a would have had no need to send you here to sound me out.''

"My God!" She looked into his face with admiring incredulity. "You're my kind of person, Maq. Trust nobody, especially your friends.''

"It's the first principle of survival," said Ancor.

"Lord, but you're ugly!" She reached up with slim green fingers and explored the intriguing texture of his face, her caress made just a little bit exceptional by the slightest tingle of mild electric stimulation. He leaned towards her, but the muskmasked scent of the pheromones in the perfume, driven by the warmth of her body, was a needless piquant: the Lion had already made up his own mind on how the conversation should be terminated. They fell to making love, and he found her deliciously shocking and shockingly delicious, and her loveplay was an altogether new experience.

* * *

Five days later the ship set down at Zin-Zan, a free-port located on the borders between Mars shell Federation territory and the independent state of Hammanite. It was here that the special ship for the expedition had been built, and where they were to equip for the journey. Maq's speciality was the selection of the small-arms and weapons they might require; Cherry was entrusted to procure the finest holo-projection equipment available; and Sine Anura's mandate was simply to secure for herself such garments, jewelry and perfumes as would enhance her skills as a seductress.

As Ancor had predicted, both Sine Anura and Cherry were heavily escorted on their respective journeys. He himself was apparently free to keep his own appointment with the local weaponmaster. He suspected but could not prove that a few eyes cautiously watched his back, but such surveillance did not worry him. He alone would be allowed to pass into the weaponmaster's presence, and whatever transpired in those bomb-proof, spy-proof and impenetrable chambers of the armoury would forever remain a secret.

He needed no announcement. As a formerly registered assassin, the personal-recognition computers would long have been pro-gramed to identify his every characteristic. Verification was a formality delayed only a little by a slight difference in speech-pattern he had picked up on his travels and its correlation with specific pollen grains extracted from his cloak. Once through the first security screen he surrendered all his weapons and was stripped for search and scanning before being given the scarlet admission-garment to cover his nakedness. Only then did the hard-eyed guardians relax, because like Ancor himself, weapon-masters left very little to chance.

Half a mile below, in a magnificent and curtained room deep in the concrete vaults, a surprise awaited him. As well as the local weaponmaster he had been expecting to meet, the familiar face of Tortigus Veritain, probably the greatest weaponmaster of them all, was there to greet him.

"It's a dangerous game you're playing, Maq," said Veritain concernedly.

Ancor grimaced. "I'll survive it, Tortigus. Given the right weapons."

"The weapons we have arranged. Our latest specialities are such that even the police hunter-killer squads haven't yet seen their like."

"I thought Federation contracts precluded you from selling hunter-killer weapons in the open market."

"They do! They do!" Veritain spread his hands expressively. "But it will be at least three years before these are even offered to the police—and the contract says nothing about weapons they've not even started to consider. So for you, there are no restrictions."

"Why should you do me such a favour, Tortigus? Don't you know I've been unfrocked?"

"Of course we know. We know also that you have friends in very high places."

"If I had such friends, I would not be at liberty to discuss them."

"Nor would we expect you to, Maq. We speak theoretically, of course. Come, take advantage of our offer. It's one not likely to be repeated."

Ancor made his selection, fascinated by the power and versatility of the new range of hand weapons. A small projector which could rapidly fire a wide range of incendiary, gas, stun, high-velocity, high-explosive and other pellets, particularly took his fancy. Not neutralisable like a photon gun, smaller and lighter than a blaster, and nearly as accurate as a chem-laser, the new device was so well conceived that he could have carried a dozen on his person without appearing even to be armed, and could have beaten a small army single handed.

Veritain obviously approved of his choice, and the deal was struck.

"You've done me proudly, Weaponmaster!" said Ancor as he prepared to take his leave.

The weaponmaster grasped his hand powerfully. "Preserve yourself, Maq Ancor! And I have something else yet to give you for your journey." He pressed a small button into Ancor's hand.

Maq examined the offering curiously. "What is it?"

"A bubble memory. I don't know its content, but its donor thought there was much in it that you might find of interest."

"Which donor?"

"I was speaking again theoretically, my friend. Had there been a donor, I too would not have been at liberty to discuss him."

By the time Ancor had returned to the ship, the expedition vessel *Shellback* had been delivered. All were unanimous that it was quite the ugliest craft ever conceived. It had about it a blocked squareness which spoke of a hideous utilitarian strength imposed without regard for style or the niceties of aerodynamics. Its multiple drives were obvious and brutish, functional in a way which made it plain that efficiency and reliability were the only gods of those who had designed it, and its weapon pods were more overtly threatening than the sting of a killer hornet.

Nor was the inside any more congenial. Apparently only grudging concessions had been made to the areas intended for human beings to work and live in. Everything else was completely dedicated to its particular task, with a single-mindedness which was numbing to contemplate. Carli, always resentful of any period of her life which had to be spent on the preparation of food, regarded the tiny galley to which she was introduced with a literal howl of horror. Nor was Cherry much better pleased with the crowded and complex cockpit from which he was supposed to operate the controls.

Only Ancor had an eye for the craft's advantages—its daunting air of durability, the excellent layout of its armaments, and the thickness of its integral shields. If he had ever doubted it, this solid tribute to Land-a's capacity for research and forethought would have been the deciding argument. The *Shellback* was loaded into the hold of Land-a's great exospheric ship, where it sat as ugly and as obvious as a spider in a bath, waiting for the moment when it would come into its own, and for some reason Ancor was forced to regard his first acquaintanceship with it as the start of the expedition proper.

CHAPTER SEVEN

Han-sa's-Arim

THE STATISTICS on Mars shell were staggering, and only tolerable because of the trick of the human mind to handle immensity only in abstract, mathematical terms. When viewed from the fringes of space, however, even the minute area of the great globe which could be seen from an altitude of five hundred miles was enough to blow the mind, and total comprehension was impossible. With a diameter of two hundred and eighty three million miles, and an equatorial circumference of eight hundred and eighty nine million miles, the surface of Mars shell was recorded as two-point-five times ten to the power of seventeen square miles, which Cherry shakily translated as two hundred and fifty thousand million million square miles.

Maq Ancor ignored the statistics and merely let the breathless impressions saturate his brain as Land-a's ship bore them through the exosphere at closing on thirty thousand miles an hour. Even at that velocity, which could only be achieved at heights where the atmosphere rivalled a good vacuum, the journey across a modest ten million mile portion of the shell to the equator would take them better than seventeen standard days, allowing for refuelling stops. It was this combination of time plus nearly unimaginable speed which stirred in Ancor's brain a subconscious appreciation of the true size of the Mars shell, and explained why exospheric travel was so viciously expensive.

For reasons of maintaining ecological and climatic balance, the gigantic terrain had been deliberately sculptured by Zeus to provide almost equal areas of land and sea. This apparently profligate squandering of potential living space had its own very powerful logic: by establishing an adequate balance of soil and atmospheric conditions, agriculture could flourish, and shell communities made self-sufficient. Thus the only continuing necessity demanded from Zeus was energy for the luminaries which drove the weather and lit and heated the lands below. This simple principle, however, vanished from recognition under the psychological impact of viewing from a great height the slow march of mountains, plains, seas and valleys. From their present altitude, even the greatest of the great shell cities could not be discerned, and even mighty oceans appeared and were passed in a few hours, seemingly inconsequential against the vast, forbidding brow of the horizon.

On the fifteenth day they came across one of the most incredible sights in the Solarian universe. What at first contact appeared to be a web-slight thread across the sky broadened to become a great and golden spear standing proud and straight from the landscape as though hurled there by some amazing god. Land-a ordered the ship's speed to be reduced so that they might have the opportunity to see it more thoroughly. It was one of the spoke-shuttle shafts reaching out across the eighty five million miles of space from the Mars shell to the Asteroid shell, through which speeded the supply and emigration shuttles by means of which Zeus regulated the affairs of Solaria.

Whilst Cherry spent his time on the *Shellback*'s flight simulator, Sine Anura had taken to sharing the observation pod with Maq, drinking in the slowly unfolding marvels of the shell on which she had lived all her life yet never before seen in such a way. She was totally enthralled with the sight of the shaft, having sometimes stood at the foot of one and watched it apparently vanish into the distance of the sky. What she had not seriously considered before was that the great shaft did not end at the point where the human eye failed to resolve it, but continued on through millions of miles of space. Seen now from five hundred miles above the surface, her perspective was completely changed, and the wonder of it lit her face with a new intensity.

"Why doesn't it fall down, Maq?" she asked.

"It doesn't fall," he said, "because it isn't quite what it seems. Although it looks solid enough, in reality it contains very little mass. It's a tubular force-field, called an Exis pi-inversion field, and what looks like solid metal is a relatively small sprinkling of atoms trapped in violent circular orbits. If you turned off the Exis field, you wouldn't get fifteen tons of dust out of the whole spoke all the way to the Asteroid shell."

"Yet the shuttles can run through it?"

"It acts as a guidepath for the shuttles, which are essentially non-guidable spacecraft in themselves. The beauty of an Exis field is that whatever is contained within it cannot react with or be acted upon by anything outside, so the shuttles experience no gravity from the mass of the shell and not even the slightest drag from the molecules in space."

"What would happen if this ship ran into it?"

"We'd crash as surely as if we'd hit a mountain. A pi-inversion field is quite impenetrable."

She was about to ask a further question when Maq leaned suddenly to the transparent dome and began to concentrate on a feature on the far horizon.

"What is it?" she asked.

"I think it's what we came for. You see there—what appears to be a flat-topped mountain range. I think that's the entrance to a cageworld."

She strained her eyes to follow the feature made slight by the distance. "It must be very high."

"It is. It has to be all of a thousand miles high if it's to do its job."

"How do you know so much about such things, Maq?"

"A good question!" Land-a had entered the observation pod silently, and there was no telling how long previously his noise-less wheels had brought him there. "My impression is that there is more to Assassin Ancor than meets the eye. For an assassin he knows too much about physics, and for a physicist, too much about killing." He made a gesture as though the subject was dismissed. "I have to give you these, Assassin Ancor."

Maq took the platelets wonderingly. "What are they?"

"The recorded results of all our researches up to date, and the best of our educated guesses on the nature and structure of the

Solarian universe. I want them updated. Cameras and recording equipment have been prepared for you, and the *Shellback*'s computer and sensors will automatically handle the routine data collection. Thus when you return, you should have turned the majority of our speculations into facts.''

"I understand.''

"As you correctly deduced, Assassin Ancor, we are approaching the entrance to a cageworld. The almanacs call the world M13, and the volcano-shaped range containing it is known geographically as Han-sa's-Arim, which roughly translates as 'Beware of the Devil's grasp.' ''

"How accessible is it?''

"Except for a craft like the *Shellback*, it's completely inaccessible. The range is over a thousand miles high, much of it sheer fused silicate and completely unscalable. Only an exospheric ship can climb above it, and at exospheric speeds, no form of exploration is possible. Furthermore, it stands in Orain territory, and although a Federation member, Orain is territorially very possessive. Thus the air-space is well guarded. We ourselves shall go no nearer than the landing pads at Bryhn, on the Hammanite-Orain borders. From then on, you're on your own.''

Bryhn was twelve hundred miles from Han-sa's-Arim, but such was the clarity of the atmosphere that it was impossible not to be permanently conscious of the great mountain dominating the scene, and even Bryhn itself was built on the early slopes which led exponentially up to the fantastic rim. From the ground, the flat top of the mighty range was not visible, and the snow-clad rise of the range blended into a shrouding cloud layer which completely obscured the view of the upper reaches. Ancor took a telescope and studied the great slopes speculatively for a long time, shaking his head with some unspoken comment.

As the *Shellback* was removed from the ship's hold, Cherry viewed the prospect with considerable unease. Although the controls of the expedition vessel had been made as simple and as foolproof as possible, twelve days spent on the flight simulator had still not given him full confidence in his ability to handle the craft, and the probability of encountering the completely unknown only seconds after struggling over the rim of a thousand mile high "volcano" did nothing to aid his peace of mind. Tez and Carli appeared to have accepted that their future was entirely in the hands of fate, and only Sine Anura still seriously searched for some means of escape, her eyes wandering longingly towards the bridges and spires of Bryhn nestling below the plateau on which the landing pads had been constructed.

Finally, Maq took charge. He had seen the inventory double checked, had himself established that all the weaponry was functioning, and become as familiar as time would allow with the capabilities and limitations both of his crew and his craft. Their farewell to Land-a was brief and completely informal, then under Cherry's quaking fingers the *Shellback* bucked and staggered into the air—and their fantastic journey had begun.

As Land-a had said, the Orainan air-space was well guarded. Territorial disputes between federated and non-federated communities were frequent, and often solved by limited force of arms. Thus it was no surprise that as they passed over the border into Orainan territory their radiation detectors lit bright with tell-tale indications of a variety of location scanning beams.

Their only advantage was that the Orainan defences initially underestimated the capabilities of the *Shellback*. From its size they apparently deduced it to be a purely atmospheric craft, and sent out some fast low-level interceptors to investigate it. Cherry was fighting hard for the height necessary to take the *Shellback* smoothly up towards the rim, and the first wave of attackers passed well below, unable to match either their altitude or their rate of climb. However, at that point Orainan defence tactics changed dramatically. A strong squadron of darts with high-altitude capability was soon clear on the screens, and the menace in their mode of approach was only too apparent.

The *Shellback* was initially at a disadvantage in not having an aerodynamic profile, and was thus hampered by drag in the heavier regions of the atmosphere. As the density of the air decreased with height, however, this penalty became less damaging to their progress, and soon they were matching their attackers' rate of climb, though still uncomfortably lacking in ground speed. With the swift, avenging darts challenging the violation of their territory, the sole factor now working in the expedition's favour must have been the unpredictable route they were taking—straight at the face of the mountain side in an apparently suicidal climb. Ancor was confident that he had armaments sufficient to fight a telling battle, but he had one serious disadvantage—Cherry was not nor ever could become an experienced combat pilot.

Soon the darts came within weapons range, and the battle was on. Having examined the *Shellback*'s capabilities, and wishing to offset his crew's complete lack of combat experience, Ancor chose not to deploy the automatic anti-missile system, but to engage instead the laser meteor defences designed for the space-going mode of travel, calculating that their present height was sufficient for these to be effective, and knowing that their response speed had to be superior to any automatic weaponry device. The pattern of explosive war-heads triggered into action harmlessly around them proved him right, but at the same time he experienced a sense of failure: no true fight was ever won by reliance on untried weapons, and the effectiveness of his defence was coincidental rather than deliberate.

Doggedly Cherry pushed the *Shellback* ever upwards towards the rim, their path being now effectively vertical as they encountered the sheer crystalline perfection of the mind-creasing walls of the higher levels. In such an attitude they were a sitting target for the ground-based missiles now beginning to rise towards them on vicious fiery tails, and it was probably only the presence of their aerial attackers which inhibited the true effectiveness of such an attack. Then the amazing *Shellback* was rising as fast as the missiles themselves could rise, and was forging into the exosphere beyond the ceiling height of the darts, and was still climbing up and up until, with a psychological sensation more shattering than vertigo, they were suddenly plunging over the broad rim of Han-sa's-Arim.

CHAPTER EIGHT

Fringeworld

THE RIM of Han-sa's-Arim was a broad annular plateau about two thousand miles in width, which ran completely round the "hole" in which the cageworld was enclosed. To the travellers in the minute *Shellback*, however, the sensations imparted by a low pass over this mighty artifact were of awe and incredulity coupled with a suddenly fearsome respect for the scale on which Zeus operated. The rim was a veritable plain of a milky, opalescent substance, which had been machined to a nearly flawless finish by the terraforming engines; and at a height of a thousand miles above the surface of the Mars shell terrain, it was effectively airless and could support no life of any kind. It had about it a quality of alienness and unreality that all of the team found unexpectedly disquieting.

Having fought to conquer the initial numbing of his mind by the impact of the scene, Ancor had torn himself away from the observation window and concentrated his attention on the activities of the *Shellback*'s computing complex. Here, as Land-a had promised, the instrument and its sensors were already busy automatically collecting and digesting all the physical data which could be acquired, and the screens were slowly filling with lines of figures which were mathematical statements about this strange environment with all the subjective human reactions to the experience completely stripped away. This made it clear, in a way Ancor had not before considered, why Land-a had also sent a human crew towards the centre of Solaria instead of merely sending an instrumented probe: figures on a screen can tell startling stories, but it takes a human being to communicate a sense of wonder.

The diameter of the cageworld had been calculated to be of the order of eight thousand miles, but Maq's figures now told him that the opening in the rim of Han-sa's-Arim was less than five thousand miles across, thus indicating that the world of M13 was well and truly "caged" in its interspace cavity deep in the thickness of the Mars shell. As they had come over the edge of the mountain and out of the rockets' range, Maq had instructed Cherry to drop their speed, and they were now moving at only a few hundred miles per hour to give him a better chance of looking for something he felt certain must exist on this featureless plain. At their current height across the rim they were too low yet to see any of the details of the great hole itself except for a slightly sharpened line on the "horizon" towards which they were heading, but Maq had the viewscreen turned to maximum magnification and was searching in front and to either side, and looking seldom towards the hole itself.

Sine Anura came and stood watching the depth of his concentration move his lion-face, slightly piqued by the loss of his company.

"What are you looking for, Maq?"

"Answers. Did you know this whole mountain is an impossibility. Even in compression there are no materials strong enough to support a mountain a thousand miles high. Under such pressures, rocks would run like water, and the whole thing would collapse under its own weight. There has to be some way for it to be done."

She wandered back to the observation window, not really understanding his concern. For her, a mountain a thousand miles high and nearly ten thousand miles across needed no explanation. It was a stark reality, as obvious as the Mars shell and the luminaries which lit it.

Finally Ancor said, "Ah!" with a little note of triumph in his voice. "I thought it might be that!"

She looked across, but from where she stood the screens were meaningless, and Ancor had already trained his cameras to automatically follow the points of his concern. Then he came to the observation bay and stood with her, and she reached out and gave his bare arm a playful little shock, to teach him that she did not like to be ignored. He grinned immensely and pulled her round to gaze deeply into her eyes. But in his eyes she could see reflected only the great white rim of Han-sa's-Arim and then the edge of the great hole which led to another world, and somehow the composite depths written in his face told of passions deeper and more enduring than any she had so far evoked in him.

Then they reached the edge of the hole, and all were fully breathless with the sight. Wrapped in white and grey and green, there hung the caged world of M13, a serene marble inlaid seemingly deep into the top of the mountain. It was a great globe wrinkled with seas and continents, its foreshortened hemisphere tucked in on all sides into the cavity in the Mars shell and separated from it by a gap of nearly a thousand miles across—the fabled interspace which was hopefully to be their route through to the centre of Solaria.

Guided by Maq's instruction, Cherry tucked the ship smartly down the edge of the rim, whilst Ancor himself returned to the computer and watched the strings of figures play across the screens. At the moment they were reading mainly the near-vacuum conditions due to the height of Han-sa's-Arim, but shortly they would encounter the interspace conditions for which the *Shellback* had reputedly been built. It was Maq's intention to sample these conditions as early as possible so that he could himself decide which, if any, level of the interspace might be even remotely tolerable to the little ship. Sine Anura's point was not lost on him that perhaps they were destined to be yet another unsuccessful trial in the series by which Land-a refined his exploratory techniques.

What the scanners did not tell him in time, and what none of them had anticipated, was the coming of the shock-wave as they entered the cavity between the cageworld and the Mars shell. Suddenly the screens went wild as they spoke of a ridge of atmospheric pressure quite unpredictable at such a height, and of atmospheric temperatures in excess of a thousand degrees centigrade. So unexpected was the phenomenon that there was no time to take the proper precautions, and the little ship staggered almost as though it had struck a solid wall. The skin temperature sensors screamed a message of alarm as the outer-most layers of the hull rose to bright, white incandescence, and then Cherry was robbed of all powers of control as mighty waves of random turbulence took the *Shellback* and tossed it like a straw in the wind.

Maq's near-instantaneous interpretation of the figures on the screens was probably the thing that saved them. Struggling through the wildly bucking corridors, which threw him cruelly about as he attempted to reach Cherry's control cockpit, he arrived bruised and shaken to reach across the illusionist's panicked hands to cut the main engine, leaving only a small thruster still in operation. Shorn of its major motive power, the ship came at once under the gravitational influence of M13, and began to lose altitude rapidly. For a while their velocity was such that the temperature of the hull actually continued to increase, but by the careful application of the retro-motors they brought their speed down to manageable proportions before they got too deeply into the stratosphere, and thus avoided the fiery "burn-out" which would have been their fate had their descent continued unchecked.

By the time they had achieved the tenuous fringes of M13's atmosphere they were well below the main region of turbulence and the ship was again responsive to the controls. With sweat streaming from his face, Cherry carefully nursed the *Shellback* into a shallow spiral flight path which finally brought them safely to a stationary position hovering only a few miles above the surface of the cageworld. It was here that they paused for a while to estimate the damage and re-assess their position.

"What the hell was that we hit?" asked Cherry shakily. His worst suspicions about the safety of the enterprise had been amply confirmed.

"I'm not sure." Ancor was checking the strain-gauges and instruments which monitored the condition of the hull. None of them registered even the slightest hint of a flaw. "But whatever it was, Land-a must have known of it, because the ship was built to take it."

Of the occupants, only Cherry, strapped in the control cockpit, had escaped without a bruise. Maq's contusions were considerable, and both Tez and Carli had been thrown about their fortunately-padded cabin-space. Initially, Sine Anura seemed to have disappeared entirely, but was then discovered safe but dazed in the centre of an automatic space-crash cocoon located in the observation bay. The first shock to the *Shellback* had thrown her against a wall, causing a superficial scalp wound and imparting a momentary concussion from which she had awoken unexpectedly immobilised by the white confines of the cocoon and vaguely wondering if she had died.

They began to look about them to discover the nature of the world they had gained. Maq's instruments told a realistic story—a breathable atmosphere, gravitation within five per cent of the Mars shell normal, and ground temperatures within the range of human tolerance. Luminaries in low orbit in the interspace provided a pattern of alternating illumination, and the massive bulk of Mars shell, now nearly a thousand miles distant, was lost in a bland neutral refraction of the atmosphere, leaving the impression that the region was infinite and undefined.

From this information they decided that the cageworld was habitable, and as the computer gave them a heading designed to take them round the cageworld to the hole on the far side of the Mars shell, they clustered around the viewports looking eagerly for the great cities they expected to find. Having been brought up on the Mars shell, where the average population density was ten thousand persons per square mile, the travellers' expectation for the two hundred million square miles of the cageworld, assuming Zeus had used the normal rule of half land and half sea, was a million million inhabitants. With living space so desperately short, it was inconceivable that Zeus would have left such a vast area unpopulated, yet they travelled fully a thousand miles without gaining sight of even a single point of habitation.

There was something faintly unnerving about the sight of such endless tracts of obviously suitable land completely without inhabitants. Here was a sea, there an isthmus, and there a vast and fertile plain sparkling with lake-chains and rivers—the arrangement was capricious and on a vastly smaller scale than the landscape of the Mars shell; yet all the essential features were assembled, and the travellers' passage over the deserted terrain was marked by a curious sense of unreality.

In an attempt to resolve the problem, Maq turned to the platelets Land-a had given to him, and inserted them into a reading slot on the computer's console. Initially the readout gave him figures for the physical parameters of the rim of Han-sa's-Arim, suggesting that there had been a similar flight at least as far as the inside of the rim, during which the data had been collected. There was no mention, however, of the shock-wave at the approach to the interspace, and many of the figures relating to M13 itself were either sketchy or marginally incorrect, as though they had been obtained by deduction rather than measurement. Either their own flight was the first to have made actual contact with the cageworld—or else any previous explorers had never returned to tell what they had found.

He was about to turn the sequence over to the computer for updating when he came across a footnote obviously entered by a human hand. It read:

> EXOSPHERIC OBSERVATION OF THE SPHERE OF M13 SUGGESTS THAT THIS IS A FRINGE-WORLD, THAT IS TO SAY A WORLD WHOSE CONSTRUCTION FELL SHORT OF A SPECIFICATION ACCEPTABLE FOR HUMAN OCCUPATION. WHILST IT IS BELIEVED THAT M13 WAS ONCE AT LEAST PARTLY POPULATED, IT IS NO LONGER LISTED IN THE SOLARIAN IDENTIFILE HEAD-COUNT, AND IS PRESUMED TO BE UNINHABITED.

"Maq," Sine Anura was on the intercom, "we're seeing some strange features on the horizon ahead. Could be something natural, but the radar returns also give us some big objects which might be buildings. Want to have a look?"

Ancor glanced at the screen ruefully. "Buildings I would doubt. But if you're seeing what I think you are, this might be a good time to prime the guns."

CHAPTER NINE

Manduval

CLOSER APPROACH proved both Ancor and Sine Anura partly wrong. There were buildings, where Ancor had thought there would be none, but they were small and obviously of a very temporary nature; whilst what Sine Anura had thought to be buildings proved to be vast earth-moving machines which were part of some major terraforming operation. For a hundred and fifty miles, a broad gash in the ground nearly a mile in width and a quarter deep showed where a new watercourse was being formed, its chasmic depths yet being completely devoid of water. The great machines, working entirely under automatic control, were now raising earth and rocks on either side to create a range of minor hills.

As remarkable as was the scale of these workings, it was

towards the curious township that the travellers' attentions were mainly directed. This appeared to have formed well to the rear of the advancing mechanical cavalcade, in the region where newly-placed topsoil had already greened with natural vegetation. A crop visually similar to rice had been planted in broad, irregular patches around the town, yet nothing about the human enclave gave any hint of permanency. It was almost as though the township settled only for the duration of a single season from planting until harvest, then moved on to follow the machines of Zeus.

Ancor had initially been concerned about these great engines. He reasoned that such was the intelligence of the great computing complex which they served that the identification of a machine like the *Shellback* in a region far from its native soil was liable to trigger some paranoid reaction by Zeus. A low pass over the giant machines, however, assured him that his fears were not justified at least in the short-term, because all the machines were dedicated to their particular tasks and none of them appeared to be equipped with armaments. Considering their immense size, he soon appreciated that they had no need for any form of weapons. Nothing, including a mountain, could have stood against them.

From the obvious panic which the close approach of the *Shellback* appeared to induce in the occupants of the township, Ancor concluded that their ship was being confused with one of Zeus' own engines. He therefore directed Cherry to land the ship at least two miles away from the town, and wait there with Tez and Carli whilst he and Sine Anura made the approach on foot. The choice of ambassadors was unarguable: both Sin and Maq were more than ordinarily capable of protecting themselves should their reception be unfavourable. Cherry was still unhappy about the arrangement, however. Although he reluctantly agreed to remain in charge of the ship, he did so only after extracting a firm promise that the pair would return within six hours without fail.

The notion that the world of M13 was outside a specification suited to human habitation was not confirmed by the experiences of Sine and Maq as they walked towards the township. It was possible that the further terraforming had already repaired the situation, but the blithe warmth, and the mild, sweet breezes were undeniably pleasant after the hot, sterile confines of the *Shellback*. The gentle hill-slopes, belying their recent formation, were rich with the grass and a variety of flowers, and the short engaging twilight of a low-orbit luminary made it one of their most memorable hours.

Their coming was detected long before they reached the town. Some workers in the fields had noticed them, and a group of children ran excitedly ahead. By the time Sine and Maq reached the outskirts, a sizeable crowd had gathered in a central clearing and someone vested with authority was already being brought to the fore to greet them.

The leader, or whatever his social role, spoke a version of standard Solarian in a curiously soft and lilting dialect which hinted at long separation of the community from the mainstream cultures. He was youthful, gave his name as Manduval, had long hair so blond as to be virtually white, and a faraway look in his eyes. His fascination with the green-tinged Sine Anura stood out like a beacon in the night.

Manduval was courteous and welcoming. He was also profoundly curious about his visitors and how they had come to this land. He seemed lost with Maq's attempt to explain the relationship between the cageworld and the Mars shell, but nodded with understanding when the ship was mentioned. Manduval said his people sometimes made their own ships to sail on water for transport and fishing, but the flying ships of Zeus were also known, and thus the idea of aerial transport was not foreign to him. He expressed great interest in seeing the *Shellback*, and Ancor promised to make an opportunity available before the team departed.

Whilst they had been talking a feast had been prepared, and a great fire lit, on which small animals were roasting, and its fiery glow and crackling sparks lit the long evening with a spirit of ancient carnival. Manduval called for wine, and taking Sine Anura by the arm, led her round the incredulous crowd and introduced her proudly to all who came near, whilst others bombarded Maq with questions or explained how harvests could only be guaranteed in the areas closely following the perpetual reworking of the terrain by the terraforming machines.

The friendly naïvety of these good-natured and philosophic people led Maq to relax slightly in their company, though from habit his attention did not wander for a moment from where Sine Anura mingled with the crowd, nor were his hands ever more than a split second away from his weapons. Then Manduval returned triumphantly with a much-flattered and laughing Sine Anura on his arm, and pressed upon his guests some bowls of heated wine.

"We must drink a toast," he said, "to the skies of Solaria, from which descend new friends as well as old enemies."

This latter reference was to the flying elements of the terraforming complexes, whose surveys completely ignored the presence of a township in the path of a proposed terrain modification, and which directed the great earth-moving juggernauts in their tasks despite the fact that their activities could completely destroy the population's only harvest for the year.

Maq tipped his bowl and drank, then reacted violently, spitting the nauseous draught back into the faces of those around him. But he was too late: some of the powerful toxins had already been absorbed and began to grip his muscles with a numb ache, and his brain seemed to reel and twist inside his skull as he, trained and formidable assassin though he was, fell to one of the oldest and most discreditable tricks in the book—poisoned wine.

When Maq woke his first reaction was to be violently sick, an exercise which sent him cold and shivering back to his foetal position on the floor. After remaining there for a while attempting to reconstruct his thoughts he forced himself to a sitting position and looked about. He was in a cell or strongroom constructed of wood, but of such strength and thickness that his unaided hands could not have secured his escape from it. Nor did he have any weapons. Whilst he had been unconscious he had been stripped completely of his clothes, and all his armaments had gone with them.

A dim light entered through a little barred grid set high in the wall, and through its mean squares Ancor could discern only the neutral blankness of the M13 sky. Then what he had judged to be a heap of sacking in the corner woke with a groan to become Sine Anura, still clothed but sick and even greener than before. He helped her to a sitting position and comforted her with a few words, but he was unable to do anything more.

The door was bolted on the other side. It was massively constructed, and studded with strong bolts of iron. Its upper half carried a small hatch on which he hammered for attention. An elderly townsman opened it and peered in, then ambled away down a corridor presumably to inform his master of the prisoners' awakening. Shortly Manduval came and looked through the hatch, and the faraway look was still present in his eyes.

"Good wakening, Maq Ancor! I am sorry about the wine, but you understand that it was necessary." His lilting voice carried a faint tone of apology.

"Necessary for whom?" asked Ancor. "I'm sure we two could well have done without it."

"Ah! But then you would not have agreed to release your ship to me. I and a couple of companions have a need for it. You are not the first to have come here and told us of the great shell of Mars. It is to there we would go, away from this cursed place."

"Don't be ridiculous! My ship is no use to you. You couldn't learn to fly it."

"I doubt I would need to," said Manduval patiently. "We have already established that there are three people still on board. Two of them I would leave here, but one of them is the flier. I offer him a trade—your lives spared in return for our passage to the great shell of Mars."

"He'd never agree to that," said Ancor positively.

"I think you're wrong, Maq Ancor. The old and skinny one was greatly concerned by your absence. Today he refuses my offer. But I think tomorrow or soon he will agree. What else should he do? Live the rest of his life out there waiting?"

"Fetch us food," said Ancor tiredly. "Else you're in danger of losing the best part of your argument."

By the time that Manduval had gone from sight, Sine had struggled to her feet, and was clutching Maq's bare shoulder for support.

"Cherry wouldn't leave us, would he?"

"He's no hero. I think he'll sit there overlong arguing with his conscience, but finally he'll go."

"And where does that leave us, Maq?"

"Rotting for the rest of our lives on M13." Ancor shook his head ruefully and looked down at his own nakedness. Never had he been more aware of his own dependence on weaponry.

Shortly some soup arrived. It served to combat the aches and nausea which still remained from the effects of the drug, and with its nourishment warming inside them, their spirits began to revive. Then Sine Anura seemed to reach a point of decision.

"I'm getting out of here, Maq," she said suddenly. "You told me that the best time to make a break was when it was least expected. Well, that time is now. If Manduval is going to Mars shell, I'm going back with him."

Ancor regarded her with a long and comprehending scowl. The anger was quiet behind his eyes.

"And what makes you think he'd be interested in taking a reptilian whore along with him?"

She smiled mockingly. "If I make a play for him, I doubt his capacity to resist."

"And you'd do that without thought for the rest of us?"

"I didn't ask to come. Nor am I the Lion's keeper."

Ancor took the rebuke silently, but moved in front of the door, defying her attempt to make contact with Manduval. She regarded his pose with savage amusement.

"You can't stop me, Maq. You may be an expert in unarmed combat, but unclothed you daren't even touch me. Six thousand volts could drop you far quicker than your reflexes could react."

He recognised the truth of this, and moved aside reluctantly.

"I could almost feel sorry for Manduval," was all he said.

Manduval himself would not have appreciated Maq's concern. When he heard that Sine Anura wished to speak with him he was delighted, because she had already been on his mind. When he heard the nature of her proposition, his joy was nearly boundless. Not even in his most erotic daydreams had he dared consider the companionship of such a compliant and desirable courtesan.

Scarcely able to believe his good fortune, he drew her towards him, his nose revelling in the unaccustomed luxury of the heady perfumes rising from the warm softness of her body. He found her not only tractable but extremely skilled in leading him into confident exploration of hitherto only half-imagined modes of stimulating love-play, and her eagerness appeared comparable to his own.

On a rising tide of passion he bore her to the couch, and was soon lunging with an ecstasy raised to a new level of experience by her muscular control and the completely generous understanding with which she nurtured his desires. As he reached the climax, the tears on his face were those of the most exquisite joy, and he was moved to shout aloud the level of his rapture.

That shout was the last sound Manduval ever made.

CHAPTER TEN

Lord of the Skies

THE FATAL shock she applied between Manduval's scrotum and his chest passed directly through his heart, and the muscular spasm threw his body completely clear of the couch. Panting, but hard-eyed and completely unrepentant, Sine Anura regained her clothes and made a quick search of the room, soon locating

Ancor's weapons in a drawer and his clothes in a cupboard. Then she was running back through the house towards the strongroom, calling loudly to Maq to prepare himself. The only man to attempt to intercept her fell with ease to her fatal fingers, and his body rolled noisily ahead of her down the wooden stairs.

Ancor took his projector through the hatch, swiftly inserted a clip of high-explosive pellets, and destroyed the main portion of the outer wall even while struggling into his clothes. Sine Anura slipped the bolts and joined him, and together they passed through the shattered wall to face the frightened belligerence of those drawn to the scene by the sound of the explosion.

The assassin's use of weaponry was effective but restrained. He first demonstrated his powers and then invited them to clear a way. Those who moved from the path escaped without harm; those who remained were destroyed by a series of crucifying blasts; and soon there was no real opposition left.

Breathlessly, the pair regained the *Shellback*, where their thankful welcome made no mention of Cherry's possible arrangement with Manduval. Nor was Sine Anura's curious about-turn discussed in public. Ancor found himself unable to decide whether she had intended to go with Manduval and then changed her mind, or whether she had planned the whole episode from the start. It was only when their little ship had resumed its journey that he sought out Sine and asked the question outright.

She was a smiling, green enigma, and in no way did her face, so rich with the guile of her Engelian ancestors, give even a hint of the emotions which rode beneath. She said: "If there is an answer to that, Maq, perhaps it has to do with your being so infernally ugly." Then she took his lion face between her hands and caressed it, and even knowing that she could have taken his life at any instant, he was glad to feel the touch of her fingers at his temples.

Ancor was conscious that on the expedition's first test of his prowess as a protector, he had failed. The apparently naïve and benign circumstances had led him to fall for a trap so obvious that he deserved not to have survived it. The more he thought about it the more obvious it became that the talents of Sine alone could have recovered them from the situation. He began to reconsider the wisdom behind Land-a's apparently incongruous choice for the composition of the group, but came to no conclusion except to achieve a vague feeling that the team was more carefully contrived than he had supposed.

In his pocket he still had the button memory given to him by Tortigus Veritain. Until this moment he had not had the leisure to explore it. Now he searched the computer panels until he found a reading aperture which would accommodate it, and sat back to watch the screen. His first encounter took him only as far as the preliminary page.

> HYPERSECURITY COMMUNICATIONS RESPONSE. ASTER FEDERATION INTELLIGENCE G25 TO PRESIDENT LAYOR. MADAM: IN ANSWER TO YOUR QUERIES REGARDING PRINCE AWA-CE-LAND-A OF THE MARS SHELL FREE STATE OF HAMMANITE, ALL SOURCES ARE IN COMPLETE AGREEMENT THAT THE PRINCE COULD NOT HAVE SURVIVED THE EXPLOSION IN WHICH HE WAS INVOLVED FIFTEEN YEARS AGO: THE ORIGIN OF THE BIONIC COMPOSITE NOW CLAIM-ANT TO THE TITLE HAS NOT BEEN EXPLAINED.

Ancor was intrigued not only by the contents of the message, but also why he should have received a copy of it. His speculations, however, were brought to an end by an urgent request from Cherry for guidance as some potentially interesting new features appeared ahead.

All this time the *Shellback* had been flying at a low altitude and moderate speed, with Tez and Sine Anura acting as observers. In this way a further five thousand miles of M13's surface had been covered, but apart from geological differences in the structure of the terrain, the features had been essentially similar: isolated pockets of human occupation co-existing in an uneasy relationship with the great terraforming forces which were literally re-shaping the whole face of the world.

The reason why M13's population was no longer listed in the Solarian Identifile had become obvious: according to Zeus this was "forbidden" territory, not currently considered suitable for human occupation, and the great machines tirelessly gouged seas and rivers and raised hills and mountains completely regardless of the human remnants who scratched a precarious living in their wake. Ancor was tempted to wonder whether the original population had been given the opportunity to emigrate, or whether they had simply been "ploughed-in" when Zeus had taken the decision to re-work the environment. There was no way of telling. Nor was it certain that Zeus was bound by "humanitarian" principles in its task of securing the maximum habitable living space for the greatest number of people.

The new features which had come into view were a number of

extremely large pyramids which were certainly of human manufacture. These were dotted on a rockbound plain, and between and around them were several straggling townships whose orientation suggested that the settlements and the pyramids were related. Terraforming operations in the area were fairly light, and the main operation in progress appeared to be the addition of topsoil which was bringing a belt of fertility in from the far horizon.

Wonderingly, they circled the area. The pyramid structures were immense, built of vast blocks of dressed stone, and obviously the work of many generations of dedicated labour. That no such similar effort had been put into the construction of the surrounding townships suggested that the pyramids had a special significance in the life of the communities. Choosing his site with care, Maq ordered Cherry to land.

Rather than attempt to approach the township, Maq decided to allow the inhabitants themselves to make the first approach. Having made touchdown, they opened the hatches, improvised a bench and some stools, and Maq, Sine and Cherry sat in the light of a low-orbit luminary whilst Carli, all the while bitching at her role, was encouraged to provide a meal and serve it outside. Only Tez remained concealed. He sat in a weapons blister, terrified by the cannons under his hands, but his presence meant that the party could assume a light and apparently innocuous pose whilst at the same time taking no unreasonable chances.

It was nearly an hour before anyone came close. Then three men similarly clad in soft, grey cotton dresses came into view, and halted for a discussion. Finally one came on alone and marched boldly towards the seated group. His manner bore the grave air of a priest. He ignored Sine and Maq, and then suddenly and unexpectedly prostrated himself before Cherry. The illusionist, clad as was his habit, in his white toga, leaped to his feet in astonishment, and looked to Maq for guidance. The latter signalled silently for Cherry to handle the conversation.

Cherry regarded the prostrate figure in front of him with considerable perplexity, then adopted his most theatrical pose and said: "I, Cherry, bid you to rise!"

The newcomer got gratefully to his feet.

"Lord, who moves the sky to thunder, we humbly welcome you. What purpose brings us this most undeserved of honours?"

"We were merely passing," said Cherry, not sure where to lead the conversation. He searched for a simplification. "We are travellers, studying many lands and many peoples."

The man's face was moved with a trace of disbelief.

"Lord of the skies, you speak strangely. Is it not written that we are the last and only ones?"

"You can't believe everything you read," said Cherry. Then he noticed Maq's cautioning frown and added hastily: "For what's written is not always perfectly understood."

The fellow's face widened with a new light. "And you could show us how to understand, O Lord?"

"I, Cherry, can bring you things more real than reality itself."

Maq Ancor intercepted rapidly. "My master has travelled far. First he would rest, and then come amongst you to show his wondrous powers. And we, his servants, would likewise wish to visit and observe. Because only through knowledge can truth be established."

The newcomer appeared only just to have noticed Ancor's formidable head, and he backed away a pace. Then his eyes roved to the green shininess of Sine Anura, and he must suddenly have believed that he was in the company of a band of angels, for he dropped to his knees with a loud cry, and was bent in supplication. When he again opened his eyes, the group was gone and the hatches of the ship were closed.

"We appear to have been given an unasked advantage," said Ancor, when the group was inside. "At the moment our information is limited, so we can't rely on it, but it would seem that Cherry has been cast in the role of a minor prophet. I intend to exploit this. I suggest that at dusk he and Carli go to the town's edge and give a holo-show using some genuine Mars shell scenes. This should give the locals plenty to think about, and if they've never seen a holo projection before, the elements of magic will be quite unmistakable."

"Any sufficiently advanced technology is indistinguishable from magic," said Cherry pompously.

Ancor ignored the remark. "Tez, I'd like you to stay on board with the guns. Should we run into trouble, a couple of s.h.e. bursts overhead should be enough to convince a primitive community like this that we're a force not to be taken lightly."

Tez shrugged his shoulders. "Where will you and Sine be?"

"Exploring. I want to try to get into one of those pyramids if possible. They're obviously much older than the town, and seem to have the status of temples. I think we could learn a lot."

Tez nodded a reluctant agreement. "But I want radio contact. If I'm to stay, I need to know what's going on."

"That's fair comment," said Ancor. "Everyone will carry arms and a radio transceiver, and keep Tez informed of their movements. Cherry, unless I misjudge the angles on that luminary, you've about an hour to put together a holo-show. Think you can make it?''

"To those of talent, nothing is impossible," said Cherry, ". . . except I'll need a hand to help me with the heavy stuff.''

As the local luminary dipped towards the horizon, the sky shaded with transient hues of red and gold and purple which would shortly fade to grey but never to complete darkness, and the early dawn of an attendant luminary was already visible at the opposite side of the sky. As the long shadows settled, however, a new light began to shine at the edge of the town, weaving a strange tale out of empty air. To the watchers' astonishment there grew on the rock-strewn plain a vision of one of the great cities of the Mars shell, but so faithfully reproduced that its existence appeared unquestionable.

"Lo, I, Cherry, bring you illusions more real than reality itself!''

Abruptly the whole scene melted and flowed in upon itself, like the recalling of strange waters, and a new vision became established: a busy market thronged by thousands and lit by a million lamps, so detailed and believable that the smell of fruits and vegetables and meats was conjured into the watchers' nostrils by their own imaginations.

Maq and Sine Anura lingered only for a short while at the edge of the spectacle. Having found acceptance by the people of the township and no anxiety about their proposal to visit the temple, they began their exploration. No guide had been asked for or offered, and in the anonymity of dusk and with all eyes watching Cherry's bright spectacular, they were alone when they climbed the dusty ramp to the aperture which led into the great pyramid itself.

On their way they had been gleaning information. The culture they had entered was agriculture-based and intensely religious in the manner of many communities who need "divine" assistance in their attempts to achieve an adequate harvest. As far back as the records could serve, Zeus had left this single plain relatively undisturbed, and their towns had not been forced to become nomadic. But whereas Maq and Sine recognised this as an accident of timing in the terraforming program, the inhabitants regarded it as proof of the power of their devotions. They prayed to Zeus and sacrificed to it every seventh child that was born. And for twenty-four generations Zeus had withheld his terrible anger and favoured them—at least, so it was written in the temples.

As they passed into the entrance of the great stone mass, Ancor heard a sudden quieting of the contact signal on the transceiver at his belt, and went out into the open again to contact the *Shellback*.

"Tez, it looks as though the bulk of this pyramid is going to block our radio signal. We intend to spend about an hour inside. Don't expect to hear from us until we come out again."

"Understood, Maq. Does Cherry know where you are?"

"We told him, but he has plenty on his mind right now."

Looking across the plain, Maq could see where a great glacial mountain was now leaping into existence, and the sight of the massive ice ridges racked with storm sent a shiver down his spine despite the warmth of the evening. Cherry's mastery of holo-illusion was undoubtedly near perfection. Ancor turned back as he heard Sine Anura calling, and there was great excitement in her voice.

CHAPTER ELEVEN

Sky Train

THEY HAD supposed from its blocklike construction that the pyramid was substantially solid and probably honeycombed with galleries. The reality was otherwise. Admittedly it appeared to have been divided into levels, each connected by broad flights of stairs, but each level occupied the entire area of the pyramid at its particular height after allowing for the massive walls and supporting pillars. They were completely astonished that such spans could be constructed using nothing more than interlocking blocks of stone, and the quality of the engineering was marvellous.

The levels were rich with religious trappings and symbols, and as they descended, each was larger than the one before. It was a conservative estimate that several times the entire population of the township could have been accommodated there at one time. Furthermore, the wear on the broad steps suggested that the pyramids were of very great age. This coincided with Maq's observation that the skills and manpower necessary for the construction of such an edifice no longer seemed to be present in the community, for the structure of the town reflected the hand of no such architects.

The whole place was lit by great brass lamps whose sputtering wicks dipped into bowls of an aromatic oil. The pungent aroma from the lamps blended with the totality of the environment, bestowing on the great halls a sense of separation from time and circumstance. It was easy to appreciate how a compelling religion could have flourished in such a place.

Around the walls, scribed deeply into the enduring stone, carvings depicted strange legends which had no meaning for the casual observer except perhaps a common theme of confrontation between great aerial ships and tall heroes gesturing defiance. So varied and imaginative were the backgrounds that Maq and Sine began to suspect that this was no local story, but one where its authors must have ranged widely across M13 or possibly even to other worlds or shells.

They made the best job they could of photographing the engravings for later interpretation, but stayed overlong at one major work in the deepest and largest hall of all. Here the scene was set with details plainly drawn but nearly incomprehensible— points linked by dotted lines and labelled with symbols, a bull, a crab, a scorpion, a plough . . . And the centrepiece, dressed in symbolic fire, was this time not a flying ship but a ball of great magnitude, which somehow reminded Maq of the immense ruby which had been inset in Land-a's platinum table. He felt that if they could understand the message of this picture they would find clues to much which they sought, but the timelessness of the place had lulled their senses, and they realised that they were long overdue to renew their contact with Tez.

They reluctantly started back up the steps, and were nearly at the top when the sound of an explosion echoed menacingly around the empty halls, shortly to be followed by a duller crash but one of such intensity that they felt the impact shake the pyramid's massive walls.

Gradually tiring of his grand expositions, which brought him no involvement other than as commentator, Cherry reduced the scale of his holo-presentations. The awe with which his activities had been regarded had placed him more nearly on the level of a god rather than a prophet, and now he worked nearer to the crowd, creating rocks from which he seemed to conjure water, and producing strange and frightening animals which he fearlessly destroyed with fire. Never before had he worked with so intent and gullible an audience, and he found the experience intoxicating.

He was therefore not pleased when Tez interrupted him on the radio. Panic edged his voice.

"Cherry I can't contact Maq because he's in the pyramid. But something's happening—up in the sky."

The wan dawn of the newly-rising luminary was now lighting the far horizon, and Cherry gave it a cursory glance, saw nothing of note, and continued with his demonstration. Tez, however, had been looking in the opposite direction, where the watchful radar screens were now brilliantly luminous with some aerial phenomena advancing slowly across the sky like iron-clad clouds.

"Cherry, can you cantact Maq? Something terrible's going to happen. I know it."

Cherry broke off and looked again, this time in the right direction. Against the wan greyness of the sky great chains of linked craft moved with a ponderous slowness on whispering engines. Part of the skyborne cavalcade was due to pass almost directly over the edge of the town and the pyramid. His audience had turned away to look also, and a vast silence had fallen over them; and from the scattered laser-light of his last exhibit Cherry could read the expression of true fear which inhabited their faces. A minute later the head of the leading chain of craft was directly overhead—and thousands of tons of finely-granulated topsoil began to filter out of the sky to bury them.

Fortunately the precipitate was well dispersed, and few on the ground were in immediate danger of being crushed or buried by it. The dry "rain" however, which piled on heads and shoulders, roofs and walls, and began to obliterate the outlines of the township, was a terrifying thing to see and experience; yet the mood of the crowd changed when they understood that whilst it would bury their houses they were not necessarily going to be killed by it. Although many had run in the initial panic, a great number had stayed, and these advanced towards the unfortunate Cherry and Carli with every sign of menace.

A great muscled fellow reached Cherry first.

"You've played us falsely, Sky Lord! Even while we watched your miracles, you call your machines to bury us."

"I didn't do it!" said Cherry. "Honest! Those things belong to Zeus, not to me."

"Command them to go away."

"I can't. They won't listen to me."

His inquisitor was incredulous. "Are you not greater than Zeus, you who can build mountains in seconds whilst Zeus takes lifetimes?"

"You don't understand," said Cherry. "It's all to do with holography . . ."

The next second he was punched to the ground, and was

half-buried by falling dirt before willing hands grabbed his spindly legs and began to haul him away. A screaming Carli was lifted bodily, and the pair were held at the head of a procession which moved purposefully out on to the plain where the falling rain of dirt was less and where a great number of people thrust about in the growing dawn-light for enough brushwood to make a sacrificial funeral pyre. Their logic was sufficient: in watching this false prophet they had angered Zeus and were now being punished. It might take many sacrifices before the deity was appeased, but what better way to seek atonement than by sacrificing those who had caused the anger?

In the ship, Tez's apprehension was nearing a frenzy. Cherry had left his transmitter working, but the sounds and fragments of conversation it collected told him nothing except that Carli and the illusionist were in trouble. The radar screens insisted that something very peculiar was happening over the town although they did not indicate its nature, and the only certainty available to Tez was that the great trains in the sky were responsible. In a voice which reflected the level of his mental agony, he again tried to call Cherry and then Maq, but received no answer. Finally, lacking other instruction, he turned the cannon on the head of the leading sky-train, and fired. The explosive burst carpeted the terrain with terrible thunder, and the great flying dirt-carrier plummeted out of the sky and fell on the pyramid itself.

When Maq and Sine finally reached the pyramid's entrance they were dismayed to find it entirely blocked by fine earth, of which more entered as they tried to clear a way with their hands. Maq immediately decided to try to clear a way with s.h.e. pellets. After four explosions he had not made much impression on the mass, but he had made a hole at the top through which they were able to crawl. More powdered earth descended before they managed to escape, but finally they were free, and Maq had seized his transceiver.

"Tez, what the devil's going on?"

"Thank God you're back, Maq!" The relief in Tez's voice was only too apparent. "I think Zeus is filling the whole plain with soil. The sky is crawling with bulk carriers, and Carli and Cherry are in trouble. I think they got blamed for the dirt-fall."

"Where are they now?"

"Out on the plain somewhere. Cherry's transmitter is still working, but he isn't using it."

"Good! I'll try to home on it. Stick with the guns, Tez, but if you have to shoot any more down try and make sure they fall short of our position."

Now the light was growing swiftly, and it was possible to see all the way to the township and to the *Shellback*, but the place was nearly unrecognisable. A dusting of brown earth already about a foot thick carpeted the entire area, and the outlines of the buildings in the town were visible only as rounded humps with the occasional flash of a yet uncovered wall. Groups of earth-dusted townsfolk were scattered about, looking remarkably form-less until they chose to run from the next major deluge of the ever-advancing trains which ran across the sky.

Possibly because the drifting earth soon rendered them as brown as their neighbours, Maq and Sine encountered neither resistance nor response as they followed the direction locator to where Cherry's transmitter had been lost and buried. Maq dug it out, and they looked round. What they had taken to be a pile of brushwood proved to be a heaped pyre with Cherry and Carli, bound hand and foot, laid like logs on top of it and now almost covered with soil. The same phenomenon which had been respon-sible for their predicament had also saved their lives, because the powdered soil had entered the pile and starved the fire of oxygen. Now the heap was dead and cold, and the attempted sacrifice had been abandoned.

As the pair were released, some of the later sky-trains were reaching the area, and these were spread more broadly than had been the first. At least one train was due to deluge the relatively clear area where the *Shellback* was located, and it was in this fact that Maq identified their real danger. For atmospheric take-off and low altitude work, the ship relied on ramjets, powerful thrusters which scooped up the atmosphere, heated it by fuel injection, and used the superheated exhaust for lift and propulsion. But no ramjet could function when its incoming air was admixed with finely powdered soil.

Shouting to Tez to try and stop the sky-trains coming, Maq literally carried Carli and supported the panicked Cherry as they made the fastest pace they could back to the ship. Tez's cannon was blasting at the head of the advancing trains, and the great flare of the explosions brought short bursts of brilliance to the otherwise dismal scene. Two of the giant carriers were halted and shook the ground like minor earthquakes when they struck, but their vastly tough exteriors and minimum of sensitive parts rendered them relatively immune to the chemical explosive Tez inexpertly hurled at them, and before the explorers had reached the ship the carriers following in the train were directly overhead.

CHAPTER TWELVE

Space-sweeper

THE *Shellback* was reluctant to become airborne, and its engines were misfiring badly, causing it to lurch and stagger alarmingly. Also a new and worrying factor had entered the saga. The carriers forming the sky-trains were separating, and no longer followed precision paths but gathered to form a steel blanket over the area where the little ship was struggling. Furthermore, it was obvious that some of the carriers were being instructed on crash-dive courses deliberately designed to crush the *Shellback*. Suddenly they had become engaged in a direct confrontation with the machines of Zeus itself.

In the flashes of light from the explosions, Maq could see where the entire population of the township was hastening towards the pyramid. This suggested that the structure historically had a function as a shelter against the less-tenable moments of Zeus' terraforming program. He knew from the size of the halls in the pyramid's base that it must have been established long before the rocky plain itself was laid, because nearly a third of it was already buried in the ground. Assuming they had provisions, and that no more than twenty feet of topsoil was now added, the townsfolk had a good chance of survival. Ancor wished them luck. He had an infinite faith in the power of human beings to survive adversity.

At that point, however, their own survival was less than certain. In addition to the hazard of occasional "suicide" dives by loaded carriers, vast tonnages of dirt were being deliberately rained upon them, and the *Shellback*'s ramjets were firing in an increasingly irregular fashion as the air-intake filters repeatedly clogged. Having clawed its way to an altitude of a hundred feet, the little ship soon became unable to maintain even this height, and stalled and dropped alarmingly, frequently staggering only a few feet above the surface and in imminent danger of crashing into the occasional boulders of rock still jutting from the earthy terrain.

Somehow Cherry managed to keep the craft airborne, and even though crippled the little ship gradually managed to outstrip its great iron antagonists, which made no attempt to follow them once they had passed beyond the edge of the hovering cloud. Fearfully, the illusionist continued to nurse the craft until the carriers appeared as little more than a fleck in the sky, then he indicated to Maq that they would have to set down to clear the filters before they dared continue.

He chose to land in a wide gully between rocky flanks. On inspection, the situation with the filters proved worse than they had feared, because some of the soil had been literally fused into the filter plates by the heat of repeated backfires. It took them ten hours of solid labour to dismantle the filters and poke the plates clean. During the time they were grounded, they took turns to monitor the radar to ensure that they were not taken by surprise by any more flying machines, but apart from slow movements on the horizon there was nothing of interest to be seen. However, when they were having a short rest before tackling the task of reassembly, Sine Anura, doing her spell at the radar, let out a sudden yell.

"Maq, there's a big one coming!"

Ancor hurled himself in through the hatch. "From which direction?"

"Straight down from above. Come and see!"

By the time he reached the screens Sine had managed to switch in the visual scanner, and the scale of the image told its own alarming story. A vast space-engine half a mile in length and with long appendages giving it the appearance of a gross metallic insect, was descending on jet thrusters so large that each pod could have contained the *Shellback* in its entirety. Even from a distance the screens showed the gigantic craft to be scarred and pitted in a way which suggested that it had seen much service in violently inclement conditions.

The sight brought to Maq's mind Land-a's quotation about devices which could bring ". . . back aggregates unimaginably large from regions where no man could possibly go." He became certain that this unwelcome visitor was one of the great space-sweepers which had assisted in the collection of the material from which the shells and cageworlds had been formed. From its trajectory, however, it was apparent that this one was after a rarer prize—it was homing on the *Shellback* itself.

Viewing the immense space-hardened appendages, obviously already aligning themselves with micrometer precision, Ancor knew that as tough as the *Shellback* was, it could never survive the ordeal. Ten toothed "grabs" each many times the *Shellback*'s size and powered to move faster than the speed of sound, would enable it to take and destroy the little craft with the ease of a cat pouncing on a mouse. With the filters still not reassembled, they had no chance of emergency flight, and even if Ancor chose to tackle it with nuclear warheads there was no guarantee he could destroy it in time. This meant he had less than six minutes in which to find an effective alternative. He was halfway through a rapid appraisal of their potential defences when his mind caught again on the unlikely composition of his team and the curious logic which had gone into its selection. Less than thirty seconds later he had reached his decision and was calling for immediate action.

Soon the immense jets of the descending space-leviathan could be plainly heard, and from the violent scream of its retromotors it was plain that it intended to hover at a height from which it could pluck its prey cleanly from the ground. Its vast bulk began to obscure the light from a passing luminary, and a long patch of shadow fell from end to end of the rocky gully in which the *Shellback* lay. Then a change took place: somehow under the ominous shade there arose the bright scene of the Solarian Circus, with the busy promenades lined with lights, and the great orbs of the exhibition halls standing proudly out against the craggy background. And somewhere in zone five the projected scene of a large fire was burning in the ruins of what had once been the hall of an illusionist named Castor.

Not really believing they could win, the crew of the *Shellback* waited fearfully for the giant steel claws to grasp and crush them. The appendages were swinging indecisively, as if thrown by a sudden conflict between its instructions and its inability to find a visual match with its quarry. For three minutes it hung there pondering, and the tension in the ship increased with each passing second. Then the great thrusters fired again and the flying juggernaut turned away towards the far horizon, leaving five people on the verge of thankful hysteria.

They were at this point roughly halfway round the cageworld, but their attitude to the journey had changed inasmuch as they now had proof that Zeus was aware of them and was antagonistic towards their progress. They were likely to meet interference any time they encountered the great machines, but Maq considered it unlikely that any of them would be armed. Mechanisms which could remove mountains or marshal asteroids would be immune to ordinary attack, and, hopefully, the *Shellback* was sufficiently unique that Zeus would have prepared no specific defence against it.

The terrain continued to pass below them virtually unchanged for well over a thousand miles, and then altered so dramatically that it left them gasping with surprise. They passed over the edge of what they had thought to be a massive cliff and found instead a hideous slope which fell fully thirty miles down to where the grey rock-ball of the mantle of M13 had literally been stripped naked in a terraforming operation of truly frightening proportions. For an area a thousand miles across, the entire crust of the planet had been completely skimmed away, and this staggering feature brought home to them more plainly than anything they had before seen on their journey, the vast scale on which the machines of Zeus had to operate when re-casting the surface of a world.

They rapidly tired of the featureless boredom of the exposed rock-ball but were humbled by its immensity. Then finally the rift was passed, and a mighty "cliff-face" rose continuously to thirty miles in height, bearing at its top the original surface of M13 which Zeus had once created and then decided to remake. Even to casual observation it was obvious why the original scheme had been a failure: here was a whole landscape, with hills and mountains, valleys and plains, yet completely lacking the one essential necessity to a species which has evolved out of the sea—water. In the whole area, not one sea or lake or river could they find, and such vegetation as existed was nothing but a dry, tindery moss.

The travellers had supposed that no habitation of such a place could ever have been contemplated, and it was therefore something of a surprise when Cherry called their attention to the presence of a vast and ruined city. Maq immediately wanted to explore it, even though, from a low pass over its crumbled roofs they soon established that it was deserted and abandoned. They made touchdown in a clearing in the centre of the city, experiencing a curious sensation of being the sole living things in an entire city of dry and dusty ghosts.

It was swiftly apparent from the size of the city that a community of perhaps several millions must have lived there for a period of many years, yet from the shape of the few roofs which remained intact it was evident that no rain had ever fallen or had even been expected. This raised the suspicion that the population must have been entirely dependent on Zeus's carriers for water: and that probably at some time Zeus found this too great a drain on its resources and discontinued the supply. For Maq the question was: had the population been removed? Or had they merely been left to die?

The answer was terrifying. From the relative abundance of

parchment skeletons, often several to a house, it was obvious that none had been given the opportunity to escape. Sometimes the disposition of the bodies suggested that fighting had taken place over a particular drinking vessel, which had probably contained a remnant of the precious fluid, but even the victor in such a fight could have achieved no more than to delay by a few hours his own final agony of death by thirst. When wandering the dust-dry streets it was all too easy to re-create in the imagination a vision of those last hours, tinged with vague, irrational hopes under a shattering blanket of hopelessness. The faith that men had had in Zeus was here betrayed, and the anguish of many millions of ghosts still lingered like a sharp scent in the arid air.

However, not all the population had gone down without a struggle. On the edge of the city there was a broad, sandy basin from which protruded a few irregular metallic shapes. Upon investigating what had been buried by the slow drift of the sand, Maq and Sine were astonished to find several of Zeus' immense terraforming engines which had been violently destroyed. In some distant past time men had quite literally declared war on Zeus, and even achieved a measurable success against the mechanisms. Whether this had happened before the enforced drought or because of it, was not apparent, but Zeus certainly knew that men could become formidable antagonists. This was perhaps why it appeared to be getting worried about a little, armed ship, commanded by a professional assassin, which was making its way in towards the centre of Solaria.

CHAPTER THIRTEEN

Hand of the Keeper

"HONESTLY, TEZ!" said Carli. "When are we going to get to this sun place anyway?"

"According to Cherry, we've still over a hundred million miles to go. Do you know, all we've done so far is go nearly round one little cageworld."

"You sound as though you're enjoying the trip."

"I'm beginning to. Land-a told them to retail his sense of wonder. That's what I'm starting to find, Carli. A sense of wonder."

"I don't sense anything wonderful about being tied up and being thrown on a bonfire whilst being covered with dirt. What's the point of it all?"

"Frontiers, Carli. Man's continuing urge to see what's over the next hill. Soon we'll reach the inner face of Mars shell—and think what sights we'll see then! People and places different from anything you could imagine."

"That's a lot of nonsense! How can there be people and places inside Mars shell. On the outside of the shell, gravity goes down—so on the inside it must go up. That must be obvious, even to you."

"It doesn't work that way." Tez was looking for some common point of agreement on which to build his explanation. "Think about this cageworld, Carli. People live 'on top' of it and 'underneath' it and all round. It's similar with Mars shell. It's as thick as a world, so that its mass creates sufficient gravity on both sides."

"Say what you like, Tez, but you'll never convince me that people live on the inside of the shell with their feet sticking upwards. It isn't natural."

Tez bit his lip. "Cherry says . . ."

"Cherry!" Her scorn reached new heights. "You can discount ninety per cent of what he says, and even the remaining ten per cent is wrong. I wish I'd had the sense to go work for Castor when he made the offer."

"Well, why didn't you, then?"

"Because . . . because . . ." She turned towards him and softened suddenly. "Because of you, you big, clumsy, adorable idiot. Don't let's argue anymore, Tez. Let's talk about the future."

He grinned broadly and gathered her into his arms.

"Hang the future! Let's talk about now."

He drew from his pocket the golden phial, still unused, which Land-a had sent to increase the pleasures of their loving. Slightly apprehensive, she allowed herself to be stripped and a cautious amount of the golden spray applied. Then all her anger and her inhibitions fled, and they entered such realism of mutual delight that even Maq and Sine might have paused in wonder.

Meanwhile, Maq was at the computer, tidying the data on M13, which they were shortly due to leave. As he summed the readout, the figures sent his mind reeling. The total area of the exterior of Mars shell was two point five times ten to the power of seventeen square miles, which was a figure which concealed its shattering enormity until you had something with which to compare it. Ancor now had that comparison, and the answers left him numb.

The cageworld of M13 had a diameter of approximately eight thousand miles, a circumference of about twenty five thousand miles, and a surface area a little over two hundred million square miles. Subjectively, M13 appeared to be big, but it was obvious that Mars shell was very much larger. How many times larger was the realisation which froze Ancor's fingers over the terminal keys. In terms of surface area—which was what living space was all about—the shell was the equivalent of one thousand two hundred and fifty million cageworlds the size of M13!

Appreciation of the figures also showed the magnitude of Zeus' problem. Land-a had said there had been one world in the beginning. "Somehow they managed to make themselves a second world, then soon had to double up and double again." How many times do you have to double up to reach a thousand million? Not a thousand times, not even a hundred. A mere thirty times is all! With the number of inhabitants roughly doubling every thirty years, the population of Mars shell alone would expand to fill the equal of a thousand million Mars shells within a thousand years.

"Maq!" Cherry was on the intercom. "We're nearly through the thickness of Mars shell. What altitude do you want held?"

"We'd better hug the surface of M13 until we're clear of the rim in case there's another shock-wave waiting up there."

"I can see the rim on the scopes, but there's a lot of other things up there also. Too distant to identify yet."

"I'm coming up to see. We know nothing about this space-region, so we daren't take chances."

As the *Shellback* made its cautious way towards the great opening which formed the exit from the cageworld's cavity to the inner face of the Mars shell, the appearance of the neutral refraction of atmosphere dwindling to near vacuum in the thousand mile width of the interspace did not alter. Only the instruments told them that the edge of the rim had been passed and that they were now looking directly into Aries-space, which separated the concentric spheres of Mars shell and Earth shell with an interval of forty-nine million miles. The scanners and radar displays, however, were more precise. The edge of the rim formed a great shadowy crescent across the face of the screens, and in the blackness which represented the space beyond, a dusting of bright spangles held station over the aperture like watchful eyes in the night.

"Zeus' reception committee, unless I miss my guess," said

Ancor. "Probably a whole flotilla of space-sweepers." He occupied himself with tuning one of the scanners to produce an enhanced image. "Yes, I thought so!"

"What do we do?" asked Cherry.

"They're obviously waiting for us, and we don't have much option but to attempt a breakthrough. Fortunately, at that distance from M13 we'll be safe in using nuclear warheads if we need to."

"Isn't there a risk of nuclear fallout on the inhabitants of the inner face of the shell?"

"That's a factor we mayn't have to worry about," said Ancor, without bothering to explain. He moved to the fire-control panel and began to arm his missiles. "When I give you a marker, take us straight over the edge there between those two sweepers, then flatten across the surface of the rim. That'll prevent them getting anything below us, so we'll only have the top and sides to worry about."

"Are they armed?" asked Cherry nervously.

"I doubt it. But we mustn't underestimate the capabilities of devices designed to catch asteroids in flight. Hopefully, our missiles will clear a sufficient gap for us to get through without us having to destroy too many."

"Why 'hopefully'?"

A thousand emotions moved across the Lion's face in a play which fascinated even the normally egocentric Cherry.

"I'm just beginning to appreciate the nature of mans' relationship with Zeus. The kept should think twice before biting the hands of their keeper."

The remark passed over Cherry's head, but he busied himself with preparations for passing out of the atmospheric mode of flight into a fast space mode. Then, on Maq's signal, the little ship leaped upwards from the surface of M13 and streaked towards the distant rim, whilst all eyes watched the progress of the cluster of great space-sweepers which hung menacingly overhead.

To an uninvolved observer it might have been possible to appreciate the "sweepers" movements as a form of three-dimensional ballet. There was a cold beauty in the grace and precision with which the giant craft ordered themselves like a flock of tidy birds of prey, each positioned for the maximum chance of a "kill", yet each allowing such separation from its neighbours that mutual interference was unlikely. And beneath its cloud of deadly predators the *Shellback* streaked low over the face of the rim like a tiny animal desperately trying to escape.

The mathematical exactitude of such a method of attack, however, played into Maq's hands. When the first of his missiles struck the most imminently dangerous of the attacking craft, two others following in close succession were unable to divert their paths, and ploughed into the disintegrating wreckage. The collision evoked a power-plant flare of such frightful intensity that the *Shellback*'s radiation shields were only just equal to the task of protecting its crew. With the leading edge of the attack blunted, Maq put two further missiles into strategic groups of the 'sweepers with similar results, then suddenly they were clear of the rim and heading down through visual darkness over the slopes of a "volcano" comparable to Han-sa's-Arim itself.

They waited anxiously to see if the attack was to be repeated. Surprisingly, not one of the 'sweepers followed them over the rim, and when they were sufficiently far fled that the great "volcano" was a mere radar shadow in the distance it was possible to see that the great craft had again congregated in a cluster and presumably had been called off from the flight.

It was then that Maq realised that Cherry was having difficulties. Even with their recent danger withdrawn, the illusionist's face was wearing the expression of a man in the middle of a nightmare who is nevertheless convinced he is fully awake. Swiftly Ancor switched in the automatic pilot, and went to Cherry's side.

"Better get yourself some rest, Cherry. That was quite a scrap while it lasted."

Cherry looked up. "It wasn't the flight. It was this . . ." He pointed through the observation window to where darkness held completely unrelieved by any luminary, and then to the scanner screens where the terrain was electronically depicted as a dull, unbroken, slightly undulating plain of rock. "No light, no atmosphere, no people, no gravity . . . nothing."

"It's a fallacy to suppose that you can populate the inside of a gravitational shell," said Ancor calmly.

"But why? The shell has roughly the same thickness as the cageworld diameter. If the cageworld can maintain gravity right round its sphere, why can't the shell maintain gravity on both faces?"

"If it were a flat plane, perhaps it might. But inside an enclosed sphere, no matter where you are, the mass of the rest of it precisely cancels out the effect at the point you are considering."

"But I have pictures . . ."

"It's one of the fictions which needed sorting from the facts, Cherry. That's why Land-a sent us here."

Cherry looked about wildly. Part of his own cherished picture of the universe had been torn completely out of his life, and he was still staggering ashen-faced under the loss. Maq helped him from the pilot's seat, and began to monitor the screens, whilst Cherry retired to his bunk not to sleep but to encourage his mind to make the adjustment.

"And I told you so!" said Carli acidly to Tez.

As the illusionist departed, Sine Anura came and stood by the pilot's cockpit.

"Cherry seems to have taken it rather hard. But you *knew*, didn't you, Maq?"

"It was postulated in Land-a's notes. Even if it hadn't been, a simple consideration of the maths would have told me the same thing."

"Then answer me a question. If there is an atmosphere on the outside of Mars shell, but none on the inside why doesn't the air come through the hole and escape into the vacuum here?"

"The answer is that a little of it does. The secret is in the height of Han-sa's-Arim, which rises to where the density of the atmosphere is less than a million millionth of that at shell level. At that height, you're getting close to a good vacuum, so that the actual air loss is only slight. But what worried me was Han-sa's-Arim and the cavity itself. By all the normal laws of physics, the mountain should have collapsed under its own weight, and the cavity been crushed out of existence. It was only when we were going over the rim that I began to see how it was done. You remember I told you about the pi-inversion field which guides the spoke-shuttles?"

"The Exis field? Yes."

"Well, the whole cageworld is formed by a spherical pi-inversion field, open only at the ends. This explains why the shell can't crush the cavity. And because the spherical field undercuts the mountain, the mountain doesn't have anything like the mass it appears to have, and a lot of the thrust is supported against the field itself. But the really beautiful point of the design is the situation of the cageworld."

"How is that beautiful?"

"Being almost entirely enclosed in the Exis field, the cageworld neither acts on nor is acted upon by the mass of the shell around it. For all practical purposes, as far as M13 is concerned, the rest of the Solarian universe doesn't exist. Can you imagine living in a universe of one?"

She ran her soft fingers through his flaring mane of hair. "Who is this ugly Lion who knows too much about physics for an assassin, too much about killing for a physicist, and too much about beauty and the art of loving to be either? One day I'll learn to understand you, Maq Ancor."

CHAPTER FOURTEEN
Fire-flash

COMPARED WITH the distances encountered on Mars shell, the forty-nine million miles of space between Mars-orbit and the Earth shell appeared to be a minor hop. The comparison, however, was deceptive. Not even the most advanced of the exospheric ships plying the shell had true space-going capability, few having the range of even a million miles without refuelling.

The *Shellback*, Ancor was finding, was fully as unique as Land-a had suggested. Its unattended power-plant was by far the smallest and most powerful Maq had ever seen. Whatever form of fuel it consumed was contained in a metal "coffin" no larger than would have been required to contain a man, and from the constant "full-power" readiness of the indicators, Ancor had come to regard the capacity of the unit as effectively infinite. The thing which worried him about a device of such sophistication was whether one whole mountain range of platinum was sufficient to pay for its development. This Land-a, who could not possibly have survived his accident, was throwing up as many questions as the whole strange universe into which he had thrust his unorthodox group of explorers.

At the *Shellback*'s rated space-mode speed of fifty thousand miles an hour, they calculated that it would take forty standard days to bring them to the vicinity of the Earth shell. Once the co-ordinates had been set into the navigation computer, the main part of the flight would be handled by the automatics, with only occasional attention from the human crew. As the little ship began to bore its way through Aries-space, Ancor had the leisure to turn again to the button memory which Tortigus Veritain had given to him. He had been hoping to find a further entry on Land-a, but the single page entry next presented made no mention of the enigmatic prince, but nevertheless provoked some thought.

AJKAVIT UNIVERSITY: PROFESSOR N.K.V. SOO
TO PRESIDENT LAYOR. MADAM: WE CAN AN-
SWER YOUR QUESTION SPECIFICALLY. THEO-
RETICAL AND EXPERIMENTAL VERIFICATION
OF EINSTEIN'S SPECIAL AND GENERAL THEO-
RIES OF RELATIVITY MAKE IT QUITE CERTAIN
THAT ACCELERATION OF A PHYSICAL BODY
TO A VELOCITY EQUALLING THE SPEED OF
LIGHT IS AN ALL-TIME IMPOSSIBILITY.

"Interesting!" said Ancor to himself. "But even more interesting is what prompted President Layor to ask the question in the
first place."

Sine Anura came in and stood behind him, reading the screen
over his shoulder.

"What does it mean?" she asked.

"It means that whilst it will take us forty days to reach Earth
shell, something travelling as fast as light could do the trip in
around four and a half minutes."

"Is that important?"

"Only if you have a really long distance to go, and only a
limited time in which to do it. If you had provisions for a year
and could travel at the speed of light, your journey could take
you nearly six million million miles. A year's journey in the
Shellback would take you only about four hundred and forty
million miles."

"So we're a whole lot slower."

"Crucially slower. If the only place you had to go was at the
distance light could travel in a year, it would take the *Shellback*
better than thirteen thousand years to make that journey. In other
words, we couldn't go."

He moved to the next entry in the button memory and received
a page of tabulated figures. These were geophysical data relating
to the Mars shell, listing the minute differences in the acceleration due to gravity at points taken from the poles to the equator.
For a minute he could not appreciate why this information had
been given to him. Then he leaned back, and every facet of his
lion-like face was involved in showing the intensity of his concern.

"Oh my bloody Christ!" he said. "The spokes!"

Sine Anura did not then get the opportunity to find out what
had provoked such an outburst. Tez was calling on the intercom.

"Maq, we can see a lot of points of light ahead. They're too
far away for the scanners to show much, but Cherry asks for you
to check them out."

"I'm on my way, Tez. Come on Sine! Let's go see what they've found."

Through the windows of the darkened observation bay the faint points of light were detectable only because of their brilliance. Even the magnified image on the scanner showed them as no more than the smallest pinpoints, and Maq had to bring the imaging up to full intensity before he began to get the information he wanted. Finally he straightened.

"It's all right. The spectro-analyses are for perfectly ordinary proto-stars. What we're seeing are the luminaries around Earth shell."

"So many?" asked Sine Anura.

"Don't forget that at this distance we're seeing a full hemisphere of the shell. I don't suppose anyone has ever seen the full half of a luminary belt at one time before."

"How unique is our situation, Maq?"

"It becomes more unique the longer I consider it. The design of the *Shellback* for instance. Land-a was perfectly right when he said that previously there were no craft available which could handle the journey. The curiosity is that there are features in the *Shellback* which I'd swear didn't result just from refinements of Mars exo-ship design. They're products of a completely new order of technology. But whose technology?"

He leant suddenly to the scanner again.

"Funny! I'd swear one of those luminaries disappeared just for a moment."

"Is that likely?"

"Well, they can't just extinguish and then re-strike. But there could be something plenty big out in space between it and us which just happened to occult it. If so, we'd best find out what it is."

He turned to the long-range radar and soon had a dozen bright blips in view, but the distances were extreme.

"Whatever they are, they're plenty big, and spread in a band about ten million miles long. Possibly some specialised Zeus craft, so we'll keep an eye on them."

For the next twenty days the tedium of uninterrupted space-flight became slowly offset by an increasing concern with the activities of the mysterious space features indicated on the radar screen. These appeared to be ranging themselves into a parabolic curve with the open end of its axis precisely aligned to anticipate the *Shellback*'s course. To test whether this arrangement was accidental or deliberate, Maq ordered several alterations in the *Shellback*'s flight plan, and always the pattern in front of them adapted to neatly enclose their projected path. There was no doubt that whatever the blips represented, they were monitoring the *Shellback*'s progress and waiting for it to arrive.

In the twenty-third day of flight, when the waiting blips were only about two million miles away, Maq began to get the first images of them on the scanner screens, but the range had to close to less than a million miles before the instrument could bring in sufficient detail to enable an identification to be made, and by this time they were already inside the open end of the parabola. As Maq straightened from the screens his face was grave.

"Not space-sweepers this time. These are different, and much larger. I suspect they're the space-keepers which fuel the luminaries. Instead of manipulators they have arrays of great pans like radar dishes, which they use to drive the clouds of fissile dust and gas from which the proto-stars are made."

"Can they harm us?" asked Sine Anura.

"I don't see how, but from the way they've taken station round us, I'd swear they're going to try."

Cherry was attempting to plot the 'keepers' position on the radar screen.

"They're all moving, Maq. Better come and see."

Ancor summed the situation hastily, bringing in the computer to help monitor the results of their interceptors' courses. Within seconds the computer predicted a complete ring constantly reducing in diameter, with the *Shellback* located at the centre.

"Damn!" said Ancor. "I've seen pictures of that ring before. It's the manoeuvre used when a new luminary is being fired up to replace one which has burned out." He readjusted the scanners quickly. "Yes, I thought so! See in the space between us and the 'keepers—that dark band. That's proto-star material being hurled in our direction."

"Is it dangerous?" asked Cherry unhappily.

"Of itself, no. It's fissile radioactive materials, but its density is so low that our radiation screens could easily withstand it. The trouble arrives when sufficient of it accretes that it begins to coalesce and achieves critical mass. When that happens, a new luminary is struck—and this one's designed with us at its epicentre."

"Hell!" Cherry began to search for a way of increasing their velocity, but Maq shook his head.

"They already have our heading figured in their calculation for the epicentre. And such is the size of the initial flare that they don't have to bother overmuch about accuracy. If we go faster or slower, the chances are we'll still finish up within range of their predictions. Our only hope is a smart turn at right angles to that disc of gas coming in.''

"Turn?'' Cherry was aghast. "Have you any idea what inertial forces would do to us if we tried to make a sharp turn at our present velocity?''

"At fourteen miles a second, it could spread us all quite thinly round the walls. But we don't have any choice. If we can't get out of range before that fire-ball strikes, it'll be instant cremation. You're strapped in the cockpit, and the other three can have a space-crash cocoon apiece.''

"What about you?''

"I'll be groaning alongside.'' He gave rapid instructions to the rest of them to take to the crash cocoons, then turned back to the illusionist at the controls. "Take us through the tightest curve you dare, Cherry. It's that or fry.''

The initial look of anxiety on Cherry's face changed to genuine anguish as the inertial force produced even by his timid course-change forced him back deeply into the padded couch, and the flesh on his face sank even more deeply than usual around his bony jaws until he looked truly like a grim skeleton at the controls. Ancor, who had been unable to find anything but the most superficial padding on which to lie, felt the massive force crushing him against the deck, and the pressures on his rib cage made even breathing difficult. Both men were aware of the grave dangers should Cherry have a black-out and be unable to maintain control, but there had been no time to program their course-change into the automatics.

From where he lay, Maq could clearly see Cherry's gaunt and haggard face, but he was unable to see the instrument panel, and was thus unable to gauge the progress of their flight. Nor was it always possible for him to determine whether Cherry was still conscious, because the forces dragging the man's skin hard against his bones would not permit any relaxation of the features. He finally achieved a dreadful certainty that Cherry must have lost control, and that they would continue to follow their vast and circular course in space either until their fuel was exhausted or they were consumed by the fiery breath of an infant luminary.

It was the fire-flash itself which resolved the situation. Even though the photo-reactive panels instantly opaqued to protect the occupants, the priming flash was obvious and undurable. There followed a period of darkness made loud by the scream of alarm systems as the biological radiation screens neared overload. These triggers must have stirred Cherry from whatever state of lapsed consciousness he had achieved, and his fingers dug convulsively into the control module clenched in his fist, and the crushing pressure eased.

Then Maq was on his feet, first assuring that Cherry was firmly in control, then hastening to the crash cocoons to see that no serious injuries had resulted. Finally he returned to the scanner and opened up the view, and the sweat beaded his brow even before the check-out figures began to emerge from the computer. Uncomfortably close to them a new proto-star lit the wastes of Aries-space, but by accident and inspiration the little *Shellback* was just in the marginal region beyond which the crucifying mix of radiation spectra could not be considered permanently damaging. Singed but otherwise intact, the stoic little vessel was already streaking on course for the remaining nineteen million miles to the great Earth shell.

CHAPTER FIFTEEN

Sky-Fellow

THE EARTH shell was smaller than Mars shell, but even so its dimensions were not inconsiderable, and its total surface area was an impressive one times ten raised to the power of seventeen square miles. If it possessed the average population density of ten thousand persons to the square mile on land covering half its surface, then the projected population for the shell was a cool figure five followed by no less than twenty zeros.

This was a figure the travellers could well have believed as they viewed the amazing cities from the air. Curiously, they found no use of exospheric ships, although there was evidence of low atmospheric flight in craft which must necessarily have ranges limited to around a thousand miles or so. Earth shell communities, it seemed, had not found the need to develop the shell-shrinking exo-craft which linked the federation on Mars shell. It was, however, a factor which worked very much in favour of the *Shellback*'s crew, because they had the high airspace to themselves and uncontested.

Having become intrigued with the geophysical data on Mars shell with which he had been presented, Ancor now wished to verify his suspicions by obtaining some similar figures for the Earth shell. He would have preferred to travel to one of the polar regions, but from the angle of their approach the nearest pole would have been a hundred and forty million miles away. He therefore designed a more modest scheme, to take sample readings more close to the shell's equator. Even so, in order to obtain any significant differences, they needed to travel several million miles, and they thrust back into the exosphere for three days of top-speed travel before Maq decided to seek a spot on which to land.

Apart from the occasional seas, they were passing mainly over relatively highly-populated regions, and here, as in similar areas of the Mars shell, the inhabitants had maximised their utilisation of the life-supporting energy from the orbiting luminaries by covering their major buildings with fields and hydroponic gardens. So successful was this policy that from high altitudes even the best of the *Shellback*'s telescopes revealed very little of the teeming millions who lived beneath and around great tracts of apparently unbroken cultivation. The scanners, however, were more precise, and could detail all the streets and thoroughfares, the parks and leisure places and all the regular features of great cities, half-hidden in the golds and greens of a vast agricultural belt.

It was the resolution of the scanners, indeed, which finally brought out the feature which caused Maq to decide where to land. Two broad mountain ranges coming together in a V, enclosed a wide tract of land in which even the scanners found only the rarest signs of habitation. Such pockets of low population density were not uncommon even on Mars shell, where the distribution of people was anything but homogeneous, and Maq had been searching for a similar feature as a way of avoiding having to explain to too many people *Shellback*'s origin or its mission.

The spot where they finally set down was completely deserted, and the others took advantage of this fact to escape the confines of the ship and bask in the warmth of an obliging luminary. Maq busied himself with his measurements and had already completed his task and transferred the results to the computer when he heard Sine Anura call urgently from the far side of the ship.

"Maq! There's a strange craft up there."

"Where?" He ducked abruptly round the *Shellback*'s bulk, then stopped almost as swiftly as if he had been shot. "I don't believe it!"

"What's the matter?"

"Nothing's the matter. I just don't believe it. That ship up there is just a big bag of gas—hydrogen probably. All used for lifting that little cabin underneath. And it has an engine which turns that big wooden screw—only they're not using it at the moment, they're drifting with the wind."

"Why should they use such a funny old thing for flight?"

"I suppose that in these regions they don't know any better. Hullo, it looks as though they're preparing to pay us a visit!"

The slowly-drifting dirigible, which had apparently cut its engine some distant off in order to make a silent approach on the light breeze, signalled its intention to stop by letting down a many-barbed anchor on a chain and waiting until this had caught in a convenient clump of trees. A rope ladder followed, and down this descended a single aviator, dressed in a suit of many-coloured leathers. The short knife at his belt had the appearance of a working tool rather than a weapon, and Maq waited easily for the strange airman to approach.

As the man neared the *Shellback* his broad face twisted into a grin.

"Greetings, sky-fellow! That's a plentifully strange ship you have there."

"No more strange than yours appears to us," said Ancor pleasantly. "Who do I have the pleasure of addressing?"

"I am Sarassim, Suzerain of Rainor. And you?"

"Maq Ancor, late of Mars shell."

"Mars shell?" Sarassim shrugged and screwed up his face. "But there are many places over the mountains of which I've never heard. What brings you to this back end of everything?"

"We're travellers seeking adventure." Maq signalled for the rest of his party to come out. "We mean no harm."

"That I can judge," said Sarassim. "Else you'd have landed inside our borders rather than just outside." He pointed to some non-apparent boundary line. "Had you come down over there, I'd have been forced to fire on you."

Ancor let the comment go without reply. The *Shellback*'s singed appearance after a close encounter with the priming flash of a newly-struck luminary was grotesque, but its ability to survive such an ordeal underscored the point that anything this primitive aviator might have flung at them was so irrelevant that even to have mentioned it would have been offensive. The Suzerain, however, was watching the others come out of the ship, and his face crinkled with wry amusement.

"So many people in such a small ship? I'll gamble you need other than gas for lifting. But if it's adventure you're seeking, you've come to the right place. The war gets more hectic by the hour."

"What war?"

"With Suzerain Karnalta, the sky-pirate from Orn. Three times this week he's raided us. But we've his measure. His forays must have cost him at least a dozen men."

"He uses ships like yours?"

"Yes, but more—many more." His eyes wandered speculatively to the green attractiveness of Sine Anura. "But this is a rare meeting. While you're here you'll surely come to my camp to fill your bellies and swap yarns with me."

"We'd be pleased to," said Ancor. "Is it far?"

"Many miles. But leave your ship here, and I'll put a guard on it. We can travel in mine. We'll be there in less than two hours."

"Are we all to come?" Tez asked Maq anxiously.

"Sure! Put a grav-lock on the *Shellback*. There'll be no force hereabouts which could take her."

Sarassim was looking at the *Shellback*, and there was a trace of envy in his voice.

"I doubt there's many who'd even want her. She's iron-frog ugly and black-burnt as though caught in a forest fire. But each of us think our own craft the noblest and the swiftest thing in the skies."

Three guards descended the precarious rope ladder, and the five travellers followed by Sarassim climbed up to take their places. The cabin of the craft was unexpected in design. What should have been windows were open slits, and there was no furniture or comforts. The plating on the wooden framework was of malleable iron, and obviously recorded the scars of many battles. Two cast cannons equipped with shot and powder constituted the major offensive weapons, although some wicked-looking crossbows appeared to Maq's weapon-trained eyes to be the more effective.

The most impressive thing in the cabin, however, was the engine. This was a large, cast-iron internal combustion device, fuelled by gas from the bags above, whose black ludicrousness shattered the air with the sound of mistimed explosions and inefficient mechanical linkages. Behind them, a giant wooden propeller, fashioned from fully half a tree, began ponderously to turn, and with the steering reins grasped firmly in his hands, Sarassim ordered the anchor to be cut adrift.

Once under way, they found the journey just clear of the tree-tops refreshingly pleasant after the confined complexities of the *Shellback*. It brought them in a little over an hour and a half to a point under a high peak where the forest terrain had been cleared of trees. It was here the Suzerain had arranged what he called his "battle-camp", and the felled timber had been usefully employed in the construction of a number of buildings to house his equipment and his men. The seven other dirigibles comprising his fleet, were initially moored there also, but most of these were despatched, presumably on patrol duties, shortly after Sarassim's arrival.

They dined in one of the larger halls, where Sarassim proved to have a natural gift as a raconteur when it came to recalling his aerial encounters with the ships of Suzerain Karnalta. The man's whole life was dominated by his twin loves of flying and fighting, and Ancor shamelessly recorded every word, knowing that the opportunity to talk with such an unlikely enthusiast might never be repeated.

Whilst they talked, the local luminary had set, and since they were in a long-sequence latitude, many hours would elapse before a new one rose to break the darkness of the night. After it was fully dark, Sarassim took them up to the tip of the peak and showed them the signal beacons which spanned the length of Rainor. One of the beacons was blinking slowly as if being obscured in some way, and Sarassim watched it carefully for a moment or two. He said nothing, but Ancor thought he detected a sudden tenseness in the man's manner as they walked back down the hill. Apart from Sarassim's own ship, the remaining dirigibles also set off noisily into the night on unstated errands.

About two hours later a messenger hurried into the hall to gasp a halting message to the Suzerain. Sarassim heard him out gravely, asked a few questions, and then turned back to Ancor.

"Something terrible has happened, sky-fellow. Karnalta's men have attacked from a quarter we'd not expected. I'm afraid they've captured your ship."

"Don't worry overmuch," said Ancor. "They can neither enter it nor do much damage to it."

"That's not the real point. I've lost best part of my battle fleet, and the area they've taken would be almost impossible to regain by fighting on the ground alone. I'm afraid that by bringing you here I've lost you your ship, and there's nothing I can do to help you regain it until I can acquire more fighting craft."

"You've one ship left—your own. And I have some special weapons. Fly me to the area and I'll make short work of Karnalta and his men."

Sarassim looked into Ancor's lion-like face and read instantly that this was no idle boast. Then he rejected the idea completely.

"It's out of the question! I've done you damage enough already. I'll not have you killed because of me. Somehow I must get some more ships." He turned and walked towards the door, pondering the problem.

Ancor caught Sine Anura's eye, and her understanding was immediate. She rose quietly and followed after Sarassim.

Some while later, the Suzerain returned, and there was a new confidence in his manner.

"Very well, sky-fellow! If you think it's worth the risk. I'll take you there. How many men do you want along?"

"None. They would only get in my way."

"You have a remarkable faith in your own powers."

"I have remarkable weapons," said Ancor coolly.

"Come to think of it, you're quite a remarkable bunch altogether." Sarassim's eyes wandered back to Sine Anura, and his face lit momentarily with some cherished recollection.

CHAPTER SIXTEEN

Mandersport

As WELL as their message-bearing function, the signal beacons seemed also to serve as navigation markers after dark, and Sarassim shrewdly read their positions and confidently set course for the area where the *Shellback* had made touchdown. When they had been travelling for a little over an hour, he stilled the thundering of the ponderous engine, and in the absolute darkness that followed, began to lower an anchor.

"We're in a good position, if there's no wind-change before first light. Now we must wait."

"What for?"

"My dear sky-fellow, you cannot fight an enemy you cannot see. That's why they struck at dusk, knowing they had the night to consolidate their position whilst we would be helpless."

"How far away are they?"

Sarassim consulted his beacons. "The nearest, probably not more than a mile downwind."

"Then let's drift towards them. We'll take them by surprise."

The Suzerain muttered something incomprehensible, but nevertheless hauled the anchor back in again.

"How long will it take to reach them?" asked Ancor.

"About eight to ten minues—not that we'll ever see them."

"We'll see them, I promise you. Now load your crossbows and stand ready. When I tell you, fire your shafts into the gasbags. That way you'll be able to salvage them later."

"And what will they be doing whilst we run so obligingly close between them?"

"They'll be occupied with other things," said Ancor.

"It's a curious way to fight a battle! You're either a madman or a genius, and only first-light will tell us which."

When he had judged the time of their drifting to be complete, Ancor took his projector and fired several star-flare pellets as near vertically into the air as the gasbags above his head would allow. The intense light thrown out by these slowly falling super-illuminants was more than adequate to light up the whole terrain, and eight moored ships were immediately visible, grouped close together though farther away than Ancor had anticipated.

"Start your engine," he told Sarassim. "And give me the steering reins."

Sarassim blinked at the marvellous glow which lit the skies, and complied without question, it suddenly occurring to him that a man who could bring his own pocket luminaries might indeed have the monopoly on surprises.

With the engine reinforcing the drift imparted by the wind, they closed rapidly on the moored ships. As the range shortened, Ancor worked swiftly. The hypersonic stun pellets he was employing had to be projected accurately through the window slits of the dirigibles' cabins if they were to be guaranteed to disable the watch-crews who would be manning them, and even one bowman or bombardier left on his feet could be sufficient to turn their attack into a disaster.

They drew near to the first vessel without any sign of their fire being returned, and Ancor knew his stun pellets had done their job. Sarassim began to use his crossbow like a man possessed, and an expression of pagan joy came upon his face. Three ships had been badly punctured by his shafts before there came the blare of a cannon from the fourth ship and the sound of heavy shot against the plating of their own cabin.

"One more like that and we're lost," said Sarassim. "They'll put the next one through our gasbag."

"Not if I have my way," said Ancor. He put a high-velocity tracer pellet straight through the offending ship, and the great fiery rosette which resulted fully confirmed his suspicions that the lifting gas was hydrogen. "Sorry to lose you a ship, Sarassim, but I didn't have much alternative."

The Suzerain started to laugh in a voice which rose to near hysteria.

"By all the gods! He takes on a whole fleet single handed, and then apologises for doing too much damage!"

They had to manoeuvre sharply back into the wind to avoid over-running the remaining craft, then three more began to sag limply under Sarassim's bowmanship. Finally the last ship dropped its anchor and turned to flee on an engine so pressed that it literally screamed.

"Shall I fetch it down?" asked Ancor.

"No. Let it run. It can carry the message of my vengeance back to those who sent it. But who will believe it? You're a terrible man, sky-fellow. I've much to thank you for, but I'll ask you not to stay too long in Rainor, because our way of life could not long survive the impact. Never think me ungrateful, but at this instant I have more sympathy for my enemies than for my ally, to whom all things seem simple."

"Hold fast to that!" said Ancor. "It is unfair that simply because of my origins I should make so easy a mockery of the combat which has occupied you for a life-time. Rest assured that by first-light we'll be gone."

Their journey was now taking them back towards the Earth shell equator, around which no less than sixteen cageworlds were located. Having no other information, the choice of precisely which cageworld they should use was determined mainly by its relative distance from their present position, and how well their course coincided with Maq's intention of collecting further geophysical data.

Their new route was not across the broad belt of fertility over which they had come, but across a series of vast plainlands separated by mountain chains set with such regularity that it was almost as if the whole area had been fashioned by some cosmic tiger's claws. Another million miles of flight, then clear on the horizon loomed the unmistakable flat-topped "volcano" which marked the entrance to a cageworld set in the Earth shell. Even from exospheric height it appeared massive and daunting, and Cherry viewed the prospect of taking the little craft over yet another "rim" with increasing apprehension. Long flights over the surface of the shell he found tolerable because the situations changed relatively slowly, but the sudden transition from high-spaceflight through to accommodating a series of unknown conditions in the cageworld interspace required a feat of mental agility he had come to dread.

At this point, however, his fears were slightly premature, because Ancor needed one more measurement from the Earth shell surface, and this had specifically to be taken at the equator.

From the equatorial line there also rose one of the great golden shafts of the spoke-shuttle system, which gathered emigrants from a wide area of the shell and sent them onwards past Mars-orbit, past the Asteroid-orbit, and on out to one of the greater shells of the outer Solarian universe, whose existence they could only infer because nobody could ever return to tell about them. From Ancor's viewpoint, the proximity of the spoke-shuttle was fortunate, because it was the centrepoint of a vast transportation network, mainly served by atmospheric aircraft, which brought in emigrants from a wide range of districts and cultures so diverse that neither the travellers nor the unusual *Shellback* would appear particularly remarkable.

Mandersport, as the complex was called, was a roofed city, whose high iron arches supported an almost continuous layer of glass over streets and buildings alike. The presence of the glass roof gave the place a quality completely unlike any other metropolis they had ever known. Every turning appeared to have its own perpetual market, and from the numbers of people resting in doorways and against walls, it appeared probable that many of its inhabitants lived and slept entirely in the streets and had no homes at all.

Taking some pieces of Land-a's platinum, which they soon converted into local currency, Sine Anura and Maq began to explore. This was the first time on their journey that they had ventured into a highly populated area, and knowing nothing of the local mores and habits, they were naturally wary. Maq had again decided that the two best able to defend themselves should make the initial trip, whilst the others remained with the ship, and it took only a short period of exposure to Mandersport to convince him that the decision was justified.

The emigration complex itself, surrounding the shuttle spoke, was the usual well-organised and quietly efficient series of halls, patrolled by armed guards and overseen by the automatic man-seeker engines. Outside of this haven of order, however, were the streets of Mandersport, where it was soon obvious that the inhabitants made their living out of the unending stream of emigrants who came to take their places in the shuttles. Because there were strict limitations on what emigrants might take with them, and no certainty that any currency they carried would be acceptable at whatever destination it was to which they would be sent, such sad travellers were easy prey for all manner of rogues

and confidence tricksters and unscrupulous merchants. A whole
industry had grown up, based on coercion, extortion, and una-
shamed theft, all of which flourished easily under the glass roofs
of Mandersport, because no enforced emigrant could have his
passage delayed whilst he made appeal to a local court, nor
could he ever return, no matter what his grievance.

Initially being mistaken for emigrants, Maq and Sine were
assailed on all sides by touts and pimps, and offered everything
from lucky charms and "Guaranteed universal Solarian currency"
to the "sex feast of a lifetime". There were even for sale
emigration-exemption dockets with the macabre advertisement of
having been issued to persons who had very recently died. On
examination, they appeared to be genuine Identifile documents,
and Ancor was darkly suspicious about the incidence of recent
deaths which had left such a range available. In any case,
identity transfer was an impossibility, and anyone gullible enough
to squander a fortune on the purchase of one of these dockets
was himself inviting a disastrous encounter with one of Zeus'
man-seeker engines.

When, from their direction and attitude, it became apparent
that the pair were not enforced emigrants, the mood of the crowd
changed from cajolery and begging to outright demands with
menace, and an unwise attempt was made to kidnap Sine Anura.
This resulted in three rogues being shocked to a point just short
of losing their lives without Maq having to intercede at all. He
found it politic, however, to wear his weapons more plainly in
view, and word soon spread that these two were dangerous, and
they were left in relative peace to continue their explorations.

Suddenly Tez's voice came through on the transceiver.

"Maq! We've trouble at the *Shellback*. They've taken Carli."

"How the hell . . . ?"

"Some fellows were talking to Cherry. He thought he was
going to get a bargain, so he opened the hatch. They jumped us,
and I got knocked out. When I woke up, Carli was gone."

"Damn! How long ago?"

"I don't quite know . . . ten, maybe fifteen minutes at a
guess. But there's no sign of her now."

Once back at the ship it was immediately apparent that they
had no means of finding just where in the whole vicious complex
of Mandersport, Carli had been taken. After a brief consideration
of the impossibility of searching the whole area, Maq turned to
Sine.

"Some of our friends out there have a surfeit of greed and
great lack of subtlety. It could just be that what they've got away

with once, they'll try again. Since they're obviously interested in womanflesh, what say we offer them some more for the taking?"

Sine Anura grinned easily. "They'll be sorry if they do."

"Maybe! But don't make them sorry too soon. We've to gamble on them taking you to the same place they've taken Carli. I'll be following."

"What makes you think they'll try it again, anyway?"

"Think carefully, Sine. In the whole of Mandersport do you ever remember seeing a woman not accompanied by a protector? It's a way of life with them."

"What do you want me to do?"

"Simply take a walk on your own from the field here into Mandersport. If you get abducted, put up a token fight but no more. I'll be with you for the final party."

So saying, he ducked out of the hatch and was soon lost to view amongst the parked craft on the field. Sine looked at Tez and Cherry, both still recovering from blows to the head, and grimaced. "Don't leave the ship, boys. If things get as rough as they threaten, our most urgent need will be for a very fast lift-off."

CHAPTER SEVENTEEN

E 12

ANCOR'S PREDICTIONS were mainly correct. Sine Anura had barely penetrated the fringes of Mandersport when a violent thrust from the front sent her spinning into an alley, where her arms were seized from behind and her wrists immediately entrapped by a wire noose which tightened more painfully the more she struggled to release it. Her not ungenuine screams brought no response from the passers-by, who plainly considered it unwise to make it any of their business. She stopped screaming when a sharp knife-point was offered to her throat from behind, and a voice said: "Less noise if you want to continue living. I can kill you as easily as take you. Don't make me carve such pretty flesh. There'll be far better uses for it in the market. Now walk!"

Sine walked, feeling the knife-point pricking at her back and soon finding herself in the midst of an escort of four ruffians who set a fast pace through the smaller ways and alleys of the

complex. That such a forced abduction could take place in full
view of the crowds and without attracting more than passing
interest was the most revealing indication she had yet had of the
all-pervading viciousness of the community. She looked about
for Maq, wondering if the incident had happened too fast for him
to have caught the action, but there was no sign of him, and no
way of knowing if he was following or not.

They came at last to a large hall which was set about with
wooden booths, some open and some curtained across. The area
was full of men, perambulating slowly, examining the contents
of the booths, and then generally passing on. Each booth contained a couch and a girl in chains and a hawker who shouted the
excellence of her bodily comforts and openly haggled about the
price. Occasionally someone in the crowd was tempted, the
hawker received his money and left, and the client would retire
behind the curtain to take the girl whether she was prepared to
accept him or not. In one of these booths, tearfully and with half
her dress torn asunder, sat Carli in her chains.

Then from the corner of her eye, Sine caught sight of Maq,
keeping a low profile in the crowd. With a nearly imperceptible
nod she indicated to him the booth in which Carli sat. She saw
Maq move slowly in that direction and heard Carli's hawker
begin his auction chant.

An empty booth was awaiting her, and her arrival had already
attracted a great deal of interest. Her abductors slipped the wire
noose from her wrists, and began to fit the chains. She waited
until she could feel the cold metal in contact, then reached out
her delicate fingers to touch the links. Two men went down
together as though they had been hit by a silent explosion, and so
inexplicable did this appear that none of the onlookers seemed to
regard her as being responsible. Then, standing unrestrained
upon the small stage on which it had been intended to display
her, Sine Anura put on her own exhibition of overt invitation,
and even the nearby hawkers left their booths and came to
watch.

Some thirty men dropped to a single hypersonic stun pellet
which Maq fired low over their heads from the rear. His next
shots were high explosives, which shattered the glass roof and
tall cast arches, and showered the whole hall with falling debris.
Then came a few moments of sheer panic and confusion, in
which most of the patrons fled, and the hawkers turned furiously
with drawn weapons to protect their interests against this savage
intrusion. Ancor dropped most of them with stun pellets, reserv-

ing his high-velocity shots for those who naïvely supposed that
the wooden booths could give them cover against his fire.

Finally, shouldering the distraught Carli, from whose limbs
still dangled short lengths of chain, Maq called out to Sine.

"Let's get out of here damn fast!"

The urgency of his tone baffled her, because Ancor was
obviously the master of the situation. However, as she ran she
saw suddenly what Maq had already seen, and her blood ran to
ice. Three of Zeus' deadly man-seeker engines were moving
swiftly into the hall . . .

"Duck!"

Initially Sine did not appreciate the exact nature of Maq's
imperative call, but she threw herself instantly on the debris-
strewn floor. There was a rapid burst of automatic firing from
one of the man-seekers, which ploughed a deep channel into an
adjacent wall, and she would certainly have been cut in half had
she remained standing. Fearfully, she looked for Ancor. He and
Carli were similarly prone, but from behind the protection of a
fallen roof-column Maq was sighting his weapon on the nearest
man-seeker. The explosion of his s.h.e. pellets in the enclosed
area of the hall was unbelievably violent and the short-tracked
death engine reared mightily and toppled on a blossom of vicious
flame.

"Run!"

There was an alleyway nearby, which, curving off to the right,
was out of the direct line of fire of the two terrible engines still
remaining. Head low, and carrying Carli in his arms, Ancor
streaked into this, and Sine Anura followed, expecting at any
second to be cut down by another burst of fire. Mercifully she
was just around the corner of the wall when the next burst came.
A few projectiles ricocheted into the alleyway, but the angle of
the entrance was too extreme for the fire to be effective.

Throwing Carli to her feet and insisting that both girls continue running, Ancor surveyed the walls adjacent to the alley's
entrance. Several major explosions shook the air, and when Sine
looked back to ascertain that Maq was following, a whole sec-
tion of a wall and part of a house was crumbling to completely
seal the entrance. Their reprieve, however, was only temporary.
The remaining man-seekers would have been programed to know
all the throughways of the complex, and would automatically
compute the strategic points from which the longer lanes could be
covered. Maq's policy of maximum speed and diversity of route,
however, appeared to be working, and for several breathless
minutes in a series of streets from which all the regular inhabi-

tants had fled, they made good progress back towards the direction of the *Shellback* on the field.

Then as they streaked across a broad lane into a smaller alley, a man-seeker which had been concealed in the alley moved out suddenly; and Maq found himself unexpectedly in face-to-face confrontation with one of the deadly engines, its high-speed machine gun only inches from his chest. Sine and Carli, who had swerved aside, saw Ancor stand there in a situation from which he had no possible chance of escape, his lion-like face looking straight into the engine's visual receptors. Then, somehow, with death only the flutter of an electron away in some decision-making circuit, Ancor gave the universe back mans' ultimate gesture of defiance. He began to laugh.

For ten incredible seconds nothing happened. The seconds lengthened into half a minute, then Maq shrugged and gestured for Sine and Carli to follow him.

"It's all right!"

Fearfully skirting the dreadful engine, Sine Anura doubled to his side.

"What did you do to it?"

"Nothing. The way I read it is that it started the attack under some local instruction, then had its orders countermanded. Every time we've been in conflict with Zeus' engines, the initial attack has never been followed up. It's as though after they've passed some crucial point in a conflict they need refer elsewhere for further powers. Fortunately, in our case, these further powers have always been denied."

"Zeus?"

"It's possible. According to Land-a's notes, Zeus is located somewhere in Venus-orbit—say thirty million miles away. Assuming the point of referment is when they make an attack and fail, it would take around five minutes for a signal to go to Zeus and back. That timing just about fits here. Unfortunately we daren't rely on it. It may only apply to individual machines."

Unaccountably, as they emerged from the buildings they could hear the *Shellback*'s hover-engines winding up, and as they ran into a clearing the little ship, already air-borne, swooped down to take them for an emergency lift-off. Ancor was about to commend Cherry for this piece of initiative, then he saw on the long-range screens the real reason for the illusionist's incentive for a quick departure. The radar horizon was bright with probably a thousand meteoroid-catching space-sweepers all moving determinedly in. Whether Cherry relished the idea or not, their only hope of escape was a crash-flight up the slopes of the "volcano" and into the cageworld interspace. Against such a massive concentration of the machines of Zeus, there was no other way.

Gamely, Cherry responded to the challenge, flinging the little craft straight up towards the rim of the mighty mountain. With nailbiting fascination they watched the space-sweepers correct their courses for an interception, but Cherry's lucky forethought in the timing of his take-off and the furious pace at which he now pushed the *Shellback* took them over the great rim a full minute before the huge mechanical predators arrived, and such was the little ship's final velocity that not even the swiftest of their pursuers could catch them.

Two thousand miles of flattened rim traversed at nearly exospheric speed took them less than three minutes to cover, then came a frightening hiatus as they plunged towards the unknown cageworld, fully fearful of what might happen if they encountered another shock-wave whilst travelling at this extreme velocity. Ironically it was probably the velocity itself which saved them. Being unable to make a sharp turn to take them back under the mountain's rim, Cherry concentrated instead on bringing the craft safely to the proximity of the cageworld in the centre of the annulus by having the craft describe a broad spiral path as he fought to reduce their speed before they encountered the atmosphere. Thus more by luck than by design they avoided the outer shock-wave region and soon, with hull temperatures rising to a visible white heat, they began to hear the scream of the cageworld's stratosphere. Far above them, many space-sweepers came out over the rim and hovered, as if watching their descent, but mercifully none followed in pursuit.

Cherry continued his spiral course until their speed was down to a few hundred miles an hour, and the surface of the cageworld was less than a mile below. Maq was already at the computer panel, watching the readouts from the ship's sensors. Except for a few respects the figures were mainly comparable with those for the Mars shell cageworld M13, with gravity, barometric pressure and atmospheric composition virtually identical. Cageworlds, it seemed, were of a standard basic pattern throughout the Solarian universe. For want of any other name Ancor entered the data collection under the heading of E12, frowning because he had no logical reason to choose this rather than any other designation.

The main respect in which E12 differed from its Mars-orbit counterpart was in its climate. The sensors told of ground temperatures well below freezing, and of great glacial ranges spread across the land. When he joined the others in the observation bay, the legend on the screens was dauntingly confirmed: in this region at least, E12 was a frozen, inhospitable wasteland, whipped by fearful winds, and with the snow and ice covering broken only occasionally where some gaunt and rocky peak stood black against a terrain so featureless and a sky so wan that it was difficult to decide where one ended and the other began.

Ancor returned to his computer and against E12 he inserted:

ANOTHER FRINGEWORLD: POPULATION UNLIKELY.

Then he sat and wondered why he found the entry so disturbing. The surface of the Earth shell was about five hundred and fifty million times that of E12, which superficially made the cageworld scarcely worth considering. Yet there was some deep reality about this great cold ball beneath them which clutched at his imagination: worlds were for living—but this one was seemingly dead.

CHAPTER EIGHTEEN

Last Men

THE FURTHER their journey continued, the more dead and desolate E12 seemed to become. Travelling at atmospheric speeds and heights, they kept a careful watch on the terrain, hoping to see some signs of life. From the incidence of ice-locked seas and oceans they estimated that, departing from Zeus' usual criteria, water occupied about seventy per cent of the total surface area, though it was mainly their instruments which told them what was frozen water and what was ice-bound land. Nowhere did they see any signs of habitation.

They found it a disheartening journey, examining the great glaciers and swooping low over ice-ridges, investigating wherever a trick of light provided a momentary illusion of colour which might betray the presence of life. Always they were disappointed. In places, vast belts of forest bearded the slopes of the higher hills, and occasionally there were runmarks in the snow which might have been made by a sled, but always proved to have been the trail of a boulder rolling down a slope, or the falling of a tree.

Maq's instruments analysed the problem. The total heat input

to the cageworld was well below the Solarian norm, because all
the local luminaries were incredibly old and had obviously not
been replaced or refuelled as would have been the case with
those over a major shell. Presumably if there was a contest for
scarce resources, Zeus adopted the logical policy of the greatest
good for the greatest number.

Reading the radiation output figures for the E12 luminaries,
Ancor virtually abandoned any hope of finding human life on the
cageworld. There was plant life in the great forest belts, and even
the great grey seas presumably supported fish, but land-based
mammalian species were either absent or present in such small
numbers that observations from the *Shellback* failed to reveal any
trace of them.

Then, when nearly eight thousand of the projected twelve
thousand miles of travel to the interior of the Earth shell had
been undertaken, Cherry made a sighting which changed their
hopes dramatically. Tired of viewing nothing but endless wastes
of ice and snow, his eyes had become peculiarly attuned to any
signs of difference, and although their height was extreme he had
seen with his unaided eyesight what the others had missed with
the telescopes—a minute series of black specks in the snow
which a low-altitude pass proved to be a pack of wolves or dogs.
Maq decided to investigate, because where a canine species
could survive, possibly the human species could survive also.

Unfortunately, after they had confirmed the sighting, the weather
turned against them, and at low altitude they were struck by a
blizzard so severe that further investigation was impossible.
They could have escaped back up to the weatherless stratosphere,
but only at the risk of losing track of this ill-defined location.
Ancor therefore decided to land and wait until the blizzard had
abated.

He left Cherry to choose the best landing site, and the illusionist opted for a position hard against a cliff-face, from the top of
whose dark bulk the wind-driven snow curled like smoke to form
an immense drift half as high as the cliff itself. In the space
between the rock-face and the drift was an area of depression,
where the snow-covering was only light and where they stood
least chance of having to dig the craft out at first-light when they
wished to continue.

Having landed, they found a curious sense of comfort in
listening to the storm from the warm womb of the *Shellback*'s
interior. Indeed so strongly did the situation appeal to them that
each half-willed himself to wake during the night to savour anew

the luxury of cosiness and security in the face of such elemental violence.

It was in the wan dreariness of first-light that Sine Anura called for Maq's attention. The blizzard had now spent its force, and in the absence of the driving wind large snowflakes curled lazily into the depression in which the ship lay.

"Maq, I may be dreaming, but I thought I saw a light."

"A light? Where?"

"Against the cliff—or in it. Just from one position when I move my head."

He followed her across the bunk, and tried to place his head where hers had been. Through the dark greys of the overcast new day, deep in the cleft in the rock below which they nestled, he saw a definite point of fire.

Instantly Maq was alert and dressing.

"I'm going out to see what it is, Sine. Everybody else wait here."

Because his ship-clothes would not have been adequate against the weather, he donned an insulated work-suit, and thrust his way out of the hatch. Dropping to the ground, he found himself nearly waist-high in uncompacted snow, and had to struggle round so that he could survey the cliff. It was so cold that his breath froze as it struck the icy air.

When he looked carefully, he could see a jagged fault in the rock-face, and a dark patch which suggested the entrance to a cave. With difficulty he forced his way towards it, and was soon rewarded by the dry, throat-catching scent of wood-smoke. From somewhere inside the recess came the deep-throated growl of a wakened dog.

"Is anybody there?" he called loudly into the depths of the cave, and advanced to where he could actually see the seat of the fire. Behind it, a dog snarled at his approach but made no movement to attack.

There was a movement from deeper in the cave, and an arm only half-seen in the dim light flung dry splinters on the fire, causing it to brighten. In its flickering illumination there stood a man dressed in a suit of ragged furs and brandishing an effective-looking spear.

"Peace to you!" said Ancor. He seated himself at the fire's edge to make it plain he had no intention of attacking. "We are travellers passing. We bring you no harm. Do you understand my words?"

The stranger came round the fire towards him, obviously unafraid, but there was a disbelief in his face as he advanced.

"I understand you. But tell us who you are, because we had thought there were no others still alive. We saw your thunderbolt descending in the storm and thought you other than men."

"That thunderbolt is nothing but a sky-ship. It takes us to many worlds and places. We found you by the merest chance. My name is Maq Ancor, and the rest of us you may meet as soon as you wish."

"They call me Anim," said the stranger gravely. He turned to introduce some others who were so far in the rear of the dim cave that Maq's eyes could not discern them. "These are my family. We are the last."

"The last of what, Anim?" asked Maq carefully.

"Before you arrived, we thought we were the last of the human race. At one time there used to be many, many others, but the weather grows more savage and colder by the year. Now I think that all the rest are dead."

"I can ease your mind on that," said Ancor. "This one world is dying, true, because your luminaries have been many centuries without attention. But elsewhere the human race thrives mightily, and populates not one world but the equivalent of millions."

"Can this be true?"

"It's true. My colleague, Cherry, would be more than pleased to show you if you've the room for him to give the demonstration."

"In the deep galleries I think there may be room. Such a thing would be a wonder to us. But even this knowledge will sustain us, for nothing breeds death like the desperate certainty that life is pointlessly ending in extinction."

"Give us an hour," said Ancor, "and we'll prove to you that extinction is the least of humanity's fears."

The deep galleries were cold, but within the range of human tolerance for those bred in them and who had a sufficient supply of covering furs. Despite the travellers' patient observations, it seemed there were local colonies of seals and even an occasional bear in the district from which warm pelts could be obtained, and below the ice there were fish enough to supplement the meat. Even deer sometimes came passing, although the herds were getting smaller every year. The effect of Cherry's holo-show on these tough but desperate survivors was a marvellous thing to see, and as the visions of far-off lands and populated places unfolded to fill the rocky cavern with fabulous sights and sounds, so Maq could understand old Anim when he broke down and wept like a child.

Finally, however, the show had to end, and the travellers returned to the ship knowing sadly there was little they could do to aid these people in their struggle for survival. It was an absolute certainty that unless the luminaries were refuelled, even the seas would eventually freeze, and all major life-forms would die an icy death. Maq had discussed the point with Anim, saying that the only way he might possibly be able to force Zeus to make the necessary maintenance would be to destroy a few of the defective luminaries completely. This carried the terrible risk of worsening the situation if Zeus did not respond.

Anim had shrugged and said: "It's a gamble worth the risk—if you can achieve it. With the way the weather is getting worse, three years will see the end of hunting and fishing, and when that happens we'll all die anyway."

Sine Anura found Ancor sitting at the screens working out the trajectories of the luminaries and running comparisons of their outputs, finally settling on one which gave out less than a tenth of the shell-face norm. He was feeding the information straight into the weaponry computer, but she knew from the look on his formidable face that he had not yet actually taken the decision to fire the weapons. Ancor could be swift and terrible in combat, but he was never wanton. Not until he had balanced all the factors of risk and advantage would he take so drastic an action.

As his fingers hovered over the final control she leant over and pressed his hand down firmly.

"It's done!" she said.

The luminary in view was grossly red and bloated, having passed into a late stage of its artificial evolution. Three nuclear warheads went into it, and the brief flare of its demise caused it to burn more hot and gloriously than it had done even in its heyday. Half a minute later the bubble of radiation collapsed and was gone save for a glowing patch of ionized contamination which hung like a cosmic ghost to mark its passing.

Ancor nodded thoughtfully and began to enter details of the event into the computer. Sine watched him carefully. "Why do you call it E12?" she asked at last.

"Just an arbitrary name. We've no almanacs to tell us any better."

"It's curious! Back in the cave those people kept calling it *the* Earth, as though it was the original from which the shell was named. Could it possibly be Land-a's one world from which it all began?"

"I don't suppose we'll ever know," said Ancor.

CHAPTER NINETEEN
Mirror Mirror

THEY CONTINUED to search carefully, but found no further signs of human habitation on E12, although it was virtually certain that other isolated pockets must exist. By no stretch of coincidence could they have alighted by accident on the sole human survivors. As they travelled, however, it became increasingly apparent that all forms of animal life were becoming extremely rare, and their major sighting was only of one small herd of deer grazing the lower edge of a forest strip.

Whilst the others continued to observe, Maq returned to the computer and ran in the geophysical data he had gained on the Earth shell. He knew before he started exactly what he would find, and the answers therefore came as no surprise. He turned again then to the button memory, and sat back to see what new thing it would say.

AJKAVIT UNIVERSITY: DOCTOR LANGOL TO PRESIDENT LAYOR.

MADAM: AS YOU HAVE RIGHTLY SURMISED, THERE IS NO ANSWER TO THE QUESTION "WHERE DO OUR EMIGRANTS GO?" OUR BEST GUESS, BASED UPON THE PREVIOUS KNOWN HISTORY OF SOLARIA IS THAT NEW SHELLS ARE STILL BEING CREATED AND POPULATED. PROFESSOR SOO, HOWEVER, HAS PRODUCED CONVINCING MATHEMATICAL PROOF THAT THE CREATION OF NEW SHELLS CANNOT CONTINUE INDEFINITELY. AT SOME POINT IN TIME THE SYSTEM MUST REACH A MAXIMUM SIZE WHICH IS DETERMINED BY THE FUNDAMENTAL LAWS OF PHYSICS. THE NEW QUESTION OF "WHERE WILL OUR EMIGRANTS GO THEN?" HAS THE MOST FRIGHTENING IMPLICATIONS.

"You can say that again!" said Ancor to himself. "But the implications are more frightening than you think!"

He signed off the computer and sat with his ponderous head in his hands in silent deliberation until Cherry called him on the intercom.

"We're nearly through the thickness of the Earth shell, Maq. So far there's no sign of anything out there waiting for us. How do you wish to play it?"

"Very fast. Wait till we're in the centre of the rim and well clear of the Exis field, then blast full strength straight up to space-mode speed. I want to minimise our chances of being caught by anything nasty which might be hiding out sight around the rim."

"Check! That'll make the space-mode run-up about fifty minutes off. Want to come and observe?"

"Not unless you need me, Cherry. I've quite a lot on my mind just now."

"Something bugging you?"

"Zeus is. It's becoming absolutely imperative we re-establish that dialogue with it."

Contrary to Maq's fears, nothing appeared to be waiting for them around the great rim which marked the exit from the E12 interspace, and they had only the briefest glimpse of the sterile inner surface of the shell before the little ship began flinging itself across the twenty six million miles of Terraven-space, headed for the Venus shell surface.

As the *Shellback* continued its build-up to space-mode speed, Ancor was on the long-range radar, watching the route ahead for possible signs of danger. He was also monitoring the communications frequencies, hoping to gain some idea of the location of Zeus by what he imagined must be its prodigious output of radio signals.

In both instances his efforts told him nothing. He was forced to the conclusion that the bulk of Zeus' communications must be routed through the spokes, outside of which they would not be detectable, and the marked absence of the machines of Zeus in Terraven-space itself, which would necessarily be using direct communication links, further robbed him of the opportunity of being able to make a guess even as to which quarter of the Venus shell hosted the computing complex which had built the Solarian universe. After nearly three weeks of spaceflight, and with the Venus shell fully in sight, he finished with no more information than he had had when the trip started.

Ancor now found himself with a problem he had not before considered: the near impossibility of finding Zeus when he did not know exactly what to look for, nor where it might be located. A detailed search of the shell was completely impractical. Even at exospheric speeds, a four hundred million mile excursion just to circumnavigate the shell would have taken the best part of a year, and although the shell's area was only around half that of the Earth shell and less than a quarter of the Mars shell, it still amassed a staggering fifty six thousand million million square miles. Unless Zeus could be induced to give away its own location, finding it could easily take a lifetime.

During the trip Ancor had spent many long hours consulting the computer, and had emerged in a state which Sine could only describe as a controlled and furious panic, and it began to take all her skill and artistry to coax him out of his dominant mood of deep preoccupation. However, when finally the Venus shell surface was only a mile or two below them he forced himself out of his introspective mood and began again to take a detailed interest in the progress of the expedition.

Superficially, the terrain of the Venus shell was similar in diversity to any of the other shells, and nothing about it even hinted that it housed Zeus on its surface. It had eleven cageworlds, and since their approach path brought them into the close proximity of one of these, the travellers made it the centre of their operations, and spent a week of interesting exploration without ever venturing more than a million miles from the giant "volcano" which gave access to the interspace through the shell. It was on one such trip that they found the "crystal temple", a building which was unusual because it appeared to have very little association with the mundane civilisations who occupied the lands around it. Sine suggested that it might be a remnant from some older culture which had now been absorbed by others, and with the memory of the intriguing carvings in the M13 pyramids as a spur, they decided to take a closer look.

They found the term "crystal" astonishingly appropriate. In some phase or accident during the creation of the shell, a vast deposit of pure quartz must have been heated to many thousands of degrees in conditions which favoured the formation of immense natural crystals of startling clarity. These, won from the shell at some later time and worked with loving care and attention, had been used both as building stones and ornaments by the artisans who had fashioned the temple. Under the rays of an obliging luminary, the whole building seemed to shine like a jewel, and the many-angled facets of the blocks trapped marvellous rainbows deep within the walls.

They landed the *Shellback* only a modest walk away, and were surprised to find their arrival attracted no attention. Indeed, as they walked towards it they began to wonder if it had been abandoned, for no guides or guardians appeared, and they had the place entirely to themselves.

Once inside, they began to have doubts about even calling it a temple, because there was no sign of anything which might be supposed to have a religious significance. Instead, it had more the appearance of a museum, containing just two rows of "exhibition cases" which were themselves nothing more than large crystal lenses polished to a rare perfection.

Passing one of these, Ancor stopped suddenly, his attention arrested by an image which the lens threw back to him. There, seemingly trapped deep in the bulk of the crystal itself, was one of the most perfect pieces of weaponry he had ever seen. Had all the weaponmasters on Mars shell pooled their knowledge and resources they could conceivably have come up with something similar, and to Ancor's experienced eyes it was obvious that the weapon was as deadly as it was beautifully conceived.

An oath from Cherry who had stopped at the lens alongside, caused Maq suddenly to wonder about the nature of the image he had in front of him, and Cherry said suddenly: "Maq, you should see this holo-projection stuff! Years ahead of anything available on Mars shell."

"Do me a favour," said Ancor quietly. "Come and look in my lens whilst I look in yours. I've a curious feeling about these exhibits."

With a shrug of non-comprehension, Cherry did as he was bid.

"What do you see now?" asked Ancor.

"More holo equipment of course. What . . . ?"

"When I looked in that one I saw a weapon. Now I see another one in yours. These damn things are reading our brains and giving us back images of what we individually regard as perfection."

By this time Carli, who had been examining spectral rainbows in the walls with Sine, came over to see what Maq and Cherry had found, and stopped entranced before one of the lenses.

"Oh, what beautiful babies!" she said. "Come and look at them, Tez."

Tez went to her side and looked. He grinned, but there was a lack of conviction in his smile.

"Aren't they beautiful?" she insisted.

"Tell us what you see, Tez," said Ancor gently.

"I see Carli, of course. It's a sort of mirror, isn't it?"

"Yes it's a sort of mirror, but of a very special kind. Apparently it reflects thoughts, not light rays. Sine, come and look in here and tell us what you see.''

Sine Anura stood before the lens and gazed fixedly, then took a step backwards, and a look of utter dread was written on her face.

"It's terrifying, Maq! All that darkness . . . swirling . . . trying to draw me in . . ."

"Darkness?" Ancor's voice reflected his surprise, but his further question was stilled by a new phenomenon. The lens itself began emitting a high-pitched tinkling sound which grew rapidly in intensity until the whole temple was filled with it, and there was something about the quality of the sound which was utterly hypnotic. The thin tintinnabulation drove all other thoughts out of their minds and even the sense of passing time was lost. Some spark of native consciousness warned Maq that the luminary was setting and that soon it would be dark, but like the others he remained transfixed by the sound, and the five of them stayed thus until the guardians of the temple came.

With the quieting of the lens, Maq passed from a dream of not knowing to a nightmare of knowing but being unable to respond. He could feel a strange web wrapped around his mind, and although ten robed and hooded figures came and divided Sine off from the rest of them, Ancor was unable to force his fingers to reach for the weapon at his hip, nor could he compel his tongue to come forth with a shout of protest.

The hooded ones had formed a circle around Sine, and with linked hands they were beginning a powerful chant. The words were an obscure mystery, but its effect on Sine was obvious and potent. She began to sway with the rhythm, and her skin became a ghastly pale as though all the life was being drawn out of her. Then she dropped to her knees with her hands clasped in front of her, looking appealingly in Ancor's direction, and the hooded ones closed in upon her with the chant rising to a new scale of triumph.

Something in Ancor's desperation found him the power to break though a little of the paralysis which bound him. He opened his mouth and gave one mighty cry of: "Wait!"

CHAPTER TWENTY

THE RING broke, and one of the hooded men came towards Ancor.

"Don't disturb yourself, my friend. It will soon be over."

"What . . . will soon be over?" Maq was fighting to regain control of his limbs, and his voice, though halting, rose loud and clear.

"The devil. She must die. She is unnatural."

"She's an Engelian. One of us. She's not a devil."

"The mirrors tell us otherwise. To preserve the human race, the beasts that breed with us must be annihilated. Else all humanity is lost."

"We're all descended from beasts," said Ancor, and his voice rolled back from the darkening vaults of the crystal ceiling.

"Granted! But her stock was never a product of nature."

"A subtlety which escapes me," said Ancor. "Leave her alone!"

From the corners of his eyes Ancor could see Sine Anura beginning to recover. His interruption had halted whatever form of pressures had been applied against her, and though her pose changed only imperceptibly, the green awareness was flooding strongly back into her face. The hooded man shrugged, as though a continuation of the argument was a waste of time, and he turned back to rejoin the ring. As the circle opened to admit him, so Sine Anura struck with the speed of a cobra, inserting herself into the ring of linked hands. Ten men dropped as one, not dead but severely shocked. And at virtually the same moment the front of the temple was shattered by a great explosion, and through the flying fragments two man-seeker engines rode swiftly in.

The sudden danger was a trigger which shook Maq completely out of his hypnotic state. His projector was in his hand, and before the man-seekers had fully cleared the glassy debris one of them was already being flung violently backwards by an s.h.e. explosion placed expertly just below its tracks. Ancor instantly dived for cover, and worked his way along behind a row of crystal lenses, trying to find a vantage point from which to attack the second engine. For a minute or so the play became a deadly game of cat and mouse between the rows of crystal lenses; then Ancor made a simple slip of timing, and for one split second was visible to the machine between two of the mirrors. The man-seeker's armaments locked him in their sights with a speed only achievable by refined servo-mechanisms, and before Ancor could possibly have fired a shot he should have been cut to pieces by high-speed projectile fire.

But nothing happened. After thirty seconds Ancor holstered his weapon and walked shakily towards the man-seeker. It remained perfectly immobile, and Ancor patted it with an expression prompted by sheer relief.

Cherry and the others, shocked by the swift transition of events, were coming out of their trance-like states. Maq signalled them urgently to follow him through the broken wall. Slightly stupefied, they came, still trying to shake the remains of the dream-state from their heads. Except for Sine Anura, who doubled to his side, her face full of puzzlement.

"Why did they say I'm unnatural, Maq? Why say I'm not a product of nature?"

"I don't know, Sine. I thought initially it was because they had never seen an Engelian before. But it wasn't their own judgement they were using. Something had been built into those lenses which signalled some difference between us. But the question arises as to why they should have bothered to develop such a thing in the first place."

"You don't think I'm an unnatural beast, do you?"

Ancor smiled. "They call me the Lion. What could be less natural than a lion who walks on two legs?"

Aboard the *Shellback* Ancor's instruments had recorded all the local signals, but it took a lengthy search before he could be certain he had identified the cryptic binary outburst by which the second man-seeker had contacted Zeus, and the answering message which had inhibited its further attack. Maq now had a clear time interval between the question and answer, and the only piece of information missing was the length of time that might have been taken for the decision before the reply had been returned. Even so, the minimum calculated distance was greater than he had expected, and he shook his head disappointedly.

He entered the figures into the computer, and set it searching its files for coincidences. In a surprisingly short time it came back with a tentative answer. The time interval between the two signal bursts was consistent with a distance of a little over one-eleventh of the shell circumference—and there were eleven cageworlds in the Venus shell. The small discrepancy in time could possibly be explained by assuming that Zeus was not located on the outer surface of the shell at all, but on the inner side of the shell adjacent to the cageworld next to the one under whose shadow they now rested.

Ancor looked at the readout without particular conviction, then finally shrugged and said: "At this point, any guesses are better than none."

This time they were under no form of attack as they approached the great rim of the "volcano", and Cherry handled the approach more confidently. In passing the inner edge of the rim, however, suddenly to see where the cageworld swum a thousand miles below them, they all again experienced that shattering sense of vertigo which was quite unlike the sensation of viewing the ground from above during normal flight. They had long accepted that no matter how many times they made such an approach they would never become used to it.

Knowing now where the regions of maximum turbulence were likely to occur, Cherry set a long slow spiral course which carried them well into the centre of the annulus, and he so reduced their speed before contact with the atmosphere that hull temperatures scarcely reached a dull red, and their progress towards this new cageworld was completely controlled.

This time Maq left the computer to digest its own data, and only to signal if what its sensors told it exceeded the preset limits of human tolerance It raised no such alarm, and the assassin was able to spend the entire period of the descent in the observation bay watching the details of the landscape gradually unfold as they dropped out of the immaculately clear sky.

Had Maq remained with the instruments, he would have learned a little earlier what his own observations finally told him: that the conditions on this world were far from uniform. As they began their atmospheric flight less than a mile above the surface, they passed first over an immense, scorched desert then immediately ran into an area of mudflats with such a sharp transition boundary that Maq was quite convinced it had to be artificial. Seeking an answer, he returned to the computer, which produced information that two adjacent belts of luminaries, whilst all in their prime and fully functional, had orbits and outputs which could have been deliberately calculated to produce a dramatic climatic change over a relatively short distance.

As if this factor was not puzzling enough, the landscape itself appeared to have been deliberately contoured in strips so as to produce even more local variations. From the cooler, moister climate which nurtured the mudflats there rose a whole block of mountains, many thrusting snow-clad peaks through the banks of transient clouds, and the high pastures were magnificently green and ablaze with coloured flowers. The idea formed suddenly in Ancor's mind that perhaps this whole world was an ecological test-bed, where the multiple lower life-forms which Zeus made available on lands and seas throughout the Solarian universe were raised and tested for their suitability to thrive in any given location.

So intriguing did they find this idea that they immediately wished to pursue it farther, and at the first opportunity Cherry brought the craft below the rising peaks to make touch-down on a high green ridge. As soon as they alighted, however, they were aware that things were not quite as they had imagined. What they had mistaken for grass proved to be a flat and hardy shrub whose rapacity for life caused it to bore into and grow directly out of the bare rock without any attendant soil, and the brilliant flowers had scimitar-broad leaves edged with splines of silica so sharp that they could easily have severed an incautious running limb. Something about the way the flowers' heads followed the movements of the travellers suggested that they were probably carnivorous, and certainly aware of passing company.

Ancor summed the situation with a frown, and his face became increasingly more thoughtful as their walk progressed. His idea about the test-bed world appeared justified, but he was having reservations about the type of location for which these specimens were intended. Near the head of the ridge Tez was attacked by a long-legged rat creature, which could run so amazingly fast that it was virtually impossible to follow its progress by eye. Fortunately Tez lost nothing but a piece of leather from his shoe, and Maq killed the rat, but only with difficulty, and thereafter they went with great caution. Then they disturbed an animal as woolly as a sheep, which turned and snarled with fierce incisors, causing Maq to keep his weapon in his hand until the creature had loped away down the hillside and gone from sight. Everything, it seemed, was well adapted for offence and defence to a level way above the norm.

"Let's get back to the ship," said Ancor finally. "There's something incredibly wrong about all this. Every damn thing here is a gross mutation."

"Is that so unexpected?" asked Sine Anura. "After all, it is an isolated cageworld. Wouldn't you expect a different chain of evolution?"

"It isn't that simple, Sine. Evolution takes time—a great deal of it. Yet nothing here is normal. It's as though the pace of evolution had been deliberately forced here."

"Is that possible?"

"Only to a limited extent. Most mutations are deleterious to the organism, and evolution occurs by natural selection of the very few mutations which confer some sort of advantage. But the things here are so far removed from the Solarian species we know, that I'd swear there hasn't been near enough time for their development to have followed a natural course."

They caught the others up at the *Shellback*'s hatch, and all turned for one last look at the magnificent peaks which rose in lofty silence to touch the random clouds. What happened then was so utterly without warning that even Maq's trigger awareness and reaction speed was insufficient to prevent it. There was a sudden swoop of shadow, the whir of great wings, a scream, and the sensation of a white canopy which spread over their heads ere sped on over a rocky cleft. Incredibly, like a great angel out of a legend, there soared a creature, half-man, half-bird, with Sine Anura clutched firmly to his muscled chest.

Ancor's weapon was ready the instant he had realised something was amiss, and he could have dropped the bird-man at any time he chose. The creature's passage immediately over the cleft, however, robbed him of the opportunity to fire, because had Sine been dropped from such a height she would most certainly have been killed. Soaring round the end of the cleft, the "angel" immediately gained height and set a course straight off across the ridges and the valleys, still tenaciously clutching his shrieking prize.

CHAPTER TWENTY-ONE

In Vitreo

THEY WATCHED the "angel" until it was fully out of sight, Ancor keeping it covered with his weapon in case it came to land and he had the opportunity to shoot without risk to Sine. Finally, however, he knew he was beaten, and his face became a terrible mask of speculation.

The incident had told him much. On this test-world not only the lower life-forms were being rapidly adapted—even men, it seemed, were not immune. In a way, it made a scary kind of sense. If fringe conditions on parts of the shells and cageworlds could not be adapted to form a suitable habitat for man, then surely it was only logical to breed men adapted to the habitat? That was probably Zeus' easiest way of achieving a high and uniform head-count. It all depended on how broadly one was prepared to spread the definition of what constituted man.

The ideas came tumbling. What was the phrase used in the crystal temple? *"The beast who breeds with us must be annihilated. Else all humanity is lost."* Sine Anura was descended from Engelian stock, and nobody had ever agreed on how her green aquatic forefathers happened to be gene-compatible with the early settlers. Now Ancor was beginning to understand. The core-stock was the same, but somehow a sub-branch of man had been adapted to populate the seas on Engle, and the dissident political settlers had arrived there quite illegally. But what would the final population have been like had this mix-up not occurred? And how many odd and out of the way spots of the Solarian universe were populated entirely by mutated strains of man?

More perplexingly, how was it achieved? The time scale for the Solarian universe, from the "one world where it all began" up to the present aggregate of shells and cageworlds, was insignificant when compared with the aeons of time required for measurable progress in evolution. Yet the aquatic Engelians were resident in their seas before the Mars shell had even been completed!

As Sine had finally disappeared from view they had flung themselves into the *Shellback*, and Cherry had set a low course which directly followed the bird-man's line of flight. This took them up into a range of jagged peaks so inhospitable that even the rapacious shrub had not bothered to grow there. Such was the complexity of the ridge-faces and clefts that a whole army of bird-men could have resided there and not been visible to a single pass from the air, nor was it even certain that the "angel" carrying Sine had not gone over the high range itself to the rocky highlands which lay beyond.

In order to cover such a complicated terrain, the little ship droned a weary search pattern back and forth over the ridges and clefts and around and occasionally over the mountain peaks, but without avail. They had seen amazing mountain "leapers", like goats but with the apparent ability of flies to climb quite vertical walls, and packs of carnivorous "sheep" in pursuit of smaller prey, but of Sine and her winged abductor they had found no trace at all. With the setting of the luminary they returned to their original ridge to wait for a new light, thinking that if Sine

managed to escape, it would be there that she would expect to
find them; but although they scanned the mountain slopes all
night with infra-red and image intensifiers, they could gain no
hope at all that she was even still alive.

For the two days following they continued the search, gradually extending the area to cover both the mud-flats on the one
side of the range and a steaming jungle swampland which irra-
tionally bordered the mountains on the other side, but found no
trace at all of Sine or the "angel". Finally Maq was forced into
a decision. That Sine had been dropped or deliberately killed was
more than a passing possibility, but even had she escaped in
some high eyrie there would have been considerable hazards in
her even attempting to descend the inclement slopes alone and
unprepared, and the vicious flora and fauna with which the place
abounded would have made it trebly unlikely that she could have
survived. Nonetheless he marked the spot where the *Shellback*
had landed, with a large stone, left a cache of provisions and
weapons, a worksuit for protection, and a note indicating that
they would come back to that point every three daylight periods
for the next twelve days in case she had returned. Then with
heavy hearts they continued with their exploration of the test-world.

As they again cleared the block of mountains and began to run
across the jungle swamps it was Carli's sharp eyes which directed their attention to one of the tracts of a river which, being
broader than average, was easily visible between the dense over-
hang of the trees. What had caught her attention was a flash of
mobile green which she had assumed to be a large fish which
had risen clear of the water and then dived again. As they
hovered for a closer look, however, the patch of green again
emerged to reveal itself as the head and shoulders of a man, even
greener than Sine Anura, who was sporting himself uncon-
cernedly in the water, leaping and diving like an able trout.
Ancor timed some of his submergences and proved beyond doubt
that they were way beyond the capabilities of any ordinary
human. He knew then that what they were seeing was something
equal to one of Sine's own aquatic ancestors, and that it was
probably from some such place as this that the watery world of
Engel had been stocked.

On the far side of the swamplands, with a division almost as
clean as if it had been cut with a knife, the terrain changed
suddenly again, giving way to another arid desert, but this one so
hot that the *Shellback*'s sensors screamed a note of warning that
the place was well out of the range of human tolerance. At first
they accelerated to cross it rapidly, believing that nothing of

interest could exist in such an inhospitable region. But they were wrong. In a central region was a water-hole, and around its meagre vegetation there were quite clearly some rude dwellings and a group of nut-brown children playing at the water's edge. It could have been a scene taken from any of the Mars shell deserts, but there was a vital difference—Maq's sensors told him that the temperature of the water in the water-hole was a scalding ninety-seven degrees Centigrade. On the hell-world for which this group was being selected, there was no chance of the accidental crossing of blood-lines with illegal settlers, because at those temperatures the settlers' blood would boil!

After three days they came back to the mountains, to find that Sine Anura still had not returned, and the cache untouched. Relatively certain now that she had died, they carried on across the swamplands and the desert to where the terrain again made a sudden and dramatic change, and fell to a great tract of modest moorland so utterly ordinary and innocuous that they were hard-put to place its position in the scheme where everything else had been subject to rigorous stress by the environment.

Sensing he had missed the point about this area, Maq opted to land, and they emerged very warily for a more thorough examination. Again they were baffled. The grasses and heathers were slightly unusual but not unique, the climate was mild, and the soil was a rich loam which proclaimed long ages of the natural cycle of vegetation and decay undisturbed by any terraforming or climatic extremes. Such was the contrast of this region with the harshness of those they knew to bound it, that Ancor was certain it had a special significance, but the point continually eluded him and he kept on sampling and testing, looking for any slight thing which might provide a clue. In the end it was the *Shellback*'s sensors which told him the one thing he had missed—vibration.

The effect was so slight that the human senses could never have detected it. The output from the transducers on the scopes showed it as a virtually imperceptible tremor, a sound conducted through the earth, but it was the wave-form which was the point of interest, the regular cyclic pattern of the operation of a vast machine. Then Ancor had his answer: the moorland was irrelevant: it was merely a covering which had grown to span a roof. In this region the important operation was taking place somewhere deeply underground.

It took them a whole day of cross-pattern searching in the *Shellback* to find the only point they could consider as an entrance. The sudden fall of the moorland to a low level left what casual inspection had supposed to be a natural cave in the hill. A closer view from the hovering craft, however, suggested that beneath the vegetative cover which had formed round the entrance there was a tunnel which was regular and certainly artificial. Ancor's enthusiasm for the find was not shared by his colleagues, who, after they had made close touchdown, showed obvious trepidation about entering such unknown premises on a world so pointedly devoted to the exploitation of living things.

Ancor respected their fears, but was himself determined to find out what strange, Satanic workshops these were which hid under the mildness of the hill. Lacking the usual brave companionship of Sine Anura, he armed himself with a powerful handlamp and weapons, donned a helmeted worksuit, established that he could maintain radio communications at least until he was well into the tunnel, then set off for the encounter alone.

The first thing he discovered was that the handlamp was unnecessary. As he penetrated the long, straight tunnel he became aware that in the vast spaces under the hill there was plenty of illumination to be found, though from its colour he judged it to be mainly ranged in the ultra-violet portion of the spectrum and not necessarily intended as lighting. As a precaution, he pulled the work-suit's photo-reactive visor over his face and added a filter, then donned the gloves he found in one of the ample pockets. If this was the workshop which produced the mutant species they had found outside, even the work-suit might only provide him with scant protection, and he was glad that it had been provided with radiation monitors.

After a quarter of a mile he was through the tunnel and into the mighty space beyond, gasping with amazement at the size and complexity of the gigantic machines he found there. Millions upon millions of little shining cells of glass were in continuous procession along endless belts, passing through unfathomable devices, entrained through furnaces and under batteries of lamps, and everywhere being divided into sub-chains which followed circular loops or were directed on to other belts which appeared to travel so far that their ends might as well have been located in infinity.

With every atom of intelligence and learning he possessed he forced his mind to try and comprehend, if only imperfectly, what these great and terrible machines were doing. After an hour, in which time he had penetrated nearly two miles and still found no sign that the place had any ending, he was beginning to build up a pattern, to recognise that certain sequences were being repeated many million times a minute, and that the products were being sorted and refined and continually passed deeper and deeper into the complex, where the volume of glass cells to be handled grew less extreme, and the processes more refined and critical.

Then at last he began to understand, and his consciousness seemed to swing on a bright needle-point as he considered the enormity of the project and its staggering conception. Even though his instincts tried to reject what his intellect was telling him, he had a dreadful certainty that he was right. To resolve his own dilemma, he tried to extract a cell from one of the swiftly moving belts, dropped it, and watched it smash against the floor, losing its vital fluids. He knelt down to examine the thing that remained in the broken glass, and his hands were shaking violently. It was a minute human foetus, still perceptibly alive.

CHAPTER TWENTY-TWO
The Human Zoo

ALTHOUGH HE had suspected what he would find, the confirmation of his fears still hit him like a staggering blow. He looked back over the two miles that he had come, then looked ahead to where the myriad belts still passed endlessly. There was no sign yet that his tour was even fully begun, and from what he had already found, he had the gravest fears about what he would discover in the rest of it.

He tested the transceiver. "Cherry—are you receiving me?"

"Faintly but sufficient, Maq. What's it like in there?"

"They haven't coined the words to describe it yet. Look, I need to go in farther. As far as I can tell I can keep a straight course from the original tunnel line, and there has to be another exit somewhere, because the whole process builds up into a climax in that direction. Can you go ahead in the *Shellback* and see if you can locate it."

Cherry's voice was dubious. "What happens if we lose communication?"

"That's a risk we'll have to take. If you find another entrance, sit there until I come. If I don't come out there, come back to your present position in twelve hours, and I'll meet you there."

"Check!" Cherry was far less than enthusiastic. "I certainly hope you know what you're doing, Maq."

"So do I, Cherry. So do I."

"So what are you doing, Maq?" he asked himself, as he turned again to follow the swift progress of the cells. "You're walking through an automatic laboratory devoted to the production of mutated life. Somehow they're building the precursors of life out of simple chemicals . . . developing long-chain molecules, nucleic acids, proteins, chromosomes . . . viable human genes . . . fertilised zygotes in artificial ova. I suspect statistically they're increasing the mutation rate by deliberately monkeying with the genes, and also randomly by radiation and mutagenic chemicals, so as to explore the widest possible range of variations of which the human organism is capable.

"Then comes the nitty-gritty bit. Most of the zygotes won't survive the mutation, and will not be viable; and out of those very few that live, even fewer will ever form a foetus and finally come to term. And even if born out of their glassy, motherless wombs, only a pitiful remnant will be adapted to survive the first few breaths of life, and only a minute fragment of those who do will carry some variation which is an advantage and not a disadvantage. And that's what this place is all about—wastage of artificial human core-stock material on a completely fantastic scale to secure an occasional mutant who—if still gene-compatible—offers to Zeus the possibility of populating some fringe zone outside the range of normal human acceptance."

He stopped for a moment, and the grim lines of his complex animal face were crossed with a momentary trace of amusement.

"And that's where a logical entity like Zeus has completely missed the point. The creation of new shells and new worlds was intended to cater for the natural increases in the existing populations. There's no sense in creating new species to populate regions the others can't inhabit. It may satisfy the head-count figures . . . but ultimately it can only make the population situation worse!"

He forgot his soliloquy then. He had reached the point where the minute foetuses were being transferred to larger, glassy wombs, each surrounded with complex devices for adding nutrients and maintaining the essential conditions for continued life. Here the running belts diverged mightily into storage bays so large that his eyes could not resolve the ends of them, because presumably artificial pregnancy required much the same duration as the purely human kind. After another mile the belts again converged, and now the soulless transparent wombs contained placentas and quite recognisable babies in foetal position, almost ready to be born. Ancor had his own reaction to the situation—he was terribly, violently sick.

Five miles farther, the birthpads were the most atrocious places he had ever seen, but he had to admit they were efficient. So, too, were the miles of sterile, self-cleaning incubators which tended the infants, of whom many were hideous, many beautiful, and many strange. Finally he came to the classification laboratory, and was forced to find a way round it, knowing that even he did not have the stomach to go in and observe. Many children entered it, and from its long, aseptic banks of instruments, very few emerged. This was an inhuman infanticide machine, dispassionately appraising its "products" and rejecting all who did not meet some projected specification. He did not see what happened to the luckless rejects, nor did he even wish to know. The effective inhumaneness of the whole project was becoming more than his mind and sympathies could bear, and dimly in the distance he could see another wall, and in that showed the welcome darkness of another door. Putting his head down, and metaphorically closing his eyes and ears to all but his own existence, Ancor ran.

As he cleared the further tunnel he could hear the drone of the *Shellback*'s engine hovering low overhead. They had not landed, and initially he wondered why. A brief look at the place he had now come to, soon explained their reticence. Here were cages and containers reminiscent of a zoo, and in each a colony, mixed in ages, exhibiting many patent variations on the human form and kind. There were giants and pygmies; skeletal men, seemingly light as gossamer; short, heavy troglodytes, probably intended for regions of high gravity; some with bulging eyes in tanks suggesting reduced air pressure; and a few with eyes deep-sunken, where the air pressure had obviously been increased. Some had no eyes at all, and were fiercely bathed in radiation, and there were a few with great self-luminous eyes who lit their own way in recesses of total darkness. Nowhere at all was normality, nor any sign that these humanoid creatures were any more than beasts and breeding stock. In a way he found it nearly as appalling as the scenes from which he had so recently escaped.

There were attendants, however, modified man-seekers for which the weapons had been replaced by extensible manipulators, moving between the "cages", tending to their charges. If these noticed Ancor at all, they gave no sign of it, and he was able to work his way undisturbed between the rows, with the *Shellback* shadowing him from above. He was looking for a sufficient clearing to allow the little craft to pick him up, but at the same time, having penetrated this far, he felt impelled to estimate as accurately as he was able, Zeus' powers and limitations in the

manipulation of human kind, and into what strange environments
it might be attempting to press these forms.

He found the range so staggering it made his head spin, but he
also gained the impression of an approaching crisis. If Zeus was
seriously intending to populate some of the extreme environments for which these creatures had been bred, then this was an
expression of a growing panic. Professor Soo had calculated that
the Solarian universe was not capable of infinite extension, and
the suggestion was that Zeus had also gained this understanding.
Here was a blatant attempt to fill every conceivable ecological
niche with organisms which would contribute to the head-count.
But there was nothing here which could ever answer the question:
"Where will our emigrants go then?"

Then, as if his shocks had not been sufficient for the day, he
was about to investigate one last cage in a series when he was
stopped by the sight of its single occupant, a sight so utterly
unexpected that Ancor momentarily wondered if he had lost his
own sanity. Surmounting a tube of shining steel sat the head and
shoulders of Land-a—only this was not Land-a, this was another
creature of similar disposition. There was no mistaking the intelligent brow or the fantastic, piercing gaze—yet here was no
recognition or any understanding. In that second Ancor had to
suddenly revise his whole conception of their mission. He knew
now that the enigma he knew as Land-a was one of Zeus'
creatures, a surrogate somehow inserted in the place of the
Hammanite prince of Mars shell who had been killed some
fifteen years earlier. But before he could consider the matter
further, Cherry swung the *Shellback* down into the gap beyond
the rows, and Ancor had to run to climb aboard.

As the craft lifted into the air, Maq began to see the full extent
of the "human zoo". They had run clear of the moorland, and
this was a flat and open area which they had previously missed;
but from the span of its cages and containers which continued for
mile after mile it was readily apparent that some of the strange
colonies were maintained through many generations before it
was decided whether the mutations were breeding true. They
supposed that the possessors of such mutations who passed this
most critical of tests were then placed in the test-bed areas for
acclimatisation and to estimate their ability to survive among the
flora and fauna developed for like conditions. What happened to
those for whom the altered genes were not dominant, Maq
hesitated to guess, but from his experience that day he knew the
end would be swift and efficient.

The others plied him with questions, but Ancor answered them with only a basic summary, particularly wishing to avoid upsetting Carli. Then, because he now felt the area had few surprises left to offer, Ancor suggested that they return to the mountain ridge where they had lost Sine Anura. Although this was a day earlier than they had promised on the note they had left for her, he had a lot of thinking to do, and the quietness of the mountain ranges appealed to him as a good situation in which to do it.

When they arrived in the mountain region it was already local dusk, and the great peaks were scarcely discernible against the clouds and mists which shrouded them. On the ridge itself, however, one single point of light stood out against the gloom, and across the high yellows of the darkening sky a single trail of smoke rose up from where a fire had been lit near the cache. They landed to find the cache and tools disturbed, but there was still no sign of Sine. They set a beacon to attract her attention if she was still in the district, then retired to their dark-sight monitors to watch the silent faces of the range.

Despite their vigilance they saw nothing, yet suddenly there came a hammering on the hatch. Weapon in hand, Ancor opened it, and there was Sine Anura, unharmed and obviously undistressed, and behind her the great "angel" who had delivered her, waving a last farewell before he rose again into the night sky and was gone from sight.

They made her comfortable and asked anxiously about her experiences, but she was reticent, almost mysterious, and had little to say except that she had stayed a few nights with an "angel". But when the others had retired, she and Maq sat talking. He told her all about the atrocious life laboratory, and she nodded her frequent agreement as he outlined his various points. Then she said seriously: "I nearly didn't come back, Maq. I think I already guessed a lot of what you've been telling me, and we know now from whence Engel was first stocked. But suddenly I felt apart . . . different from the rest of you . . . 'Unnatural', as they said in the crystal temple."

"That wasn't justified, Sine. All life started somewhere in the sea, and the line of mans' evolution runs through reptiles and primitive mammals to monkeys and apes right up to modern man. We're all part fish, part reptile, and part beast, and man is nothing but a gene's overwhelming determination to survive a series of organic and climatic accidents. And so, my dear, are you. But this is something you know as well as I. So what did fetch you back to us, Mistress Sin?"

She smiled, and suddenly all the trauma and the tears fled

away. She reached out soft green fingers to stroke his complex face.

"Maq, did you ever try making love halfway up a mountain? And where the eiderdown was the exclusive property of your partner?"

CHAPTER TWENTY-THREE
Syntax

NOW THE tensions were rising. Once they had left the test-world and gained the inner surface of the Venus shell, the indications were that they would be in the vicinity of Zeus itself; and across one final stretch of space which Land-a's notes called Hermes-space, lay the innermost shell of the Solarian universe—the shell of Mercury. Beyond that, what? Cherry's notion of a great, black singularity; or Land-a's sun which first breathed life into all mankind?

As the *Shellback* continued its progress around the test-world, Ancor turned to a consideration of Land-a's role in the inception of the expedition. He was now certain that Land-a was a mutant, but unsure as to what, apart from the necessity for continuing life-support, was the nature of the adapted speciality. On a hunch he turned to the computer's encyclopaedic files and keyed the entry for the prince's own biography.

Awa-Ce-Land-a was recorded as having suffered from acute anterior poliomyelitis since shortly after birth, and having come to maturity both with deformities and having to spend his life in an "iron lung". One look at the photograph, however, convinced Ancor that the records were mistaken. From the stern intelligence of the brow and the piercing gaze, he knew that even the original prince who had been killed in an explosion had been one of Zeus' creatures, and he suspected that there had probably been several more before him. Could it then really have been an accident that all the platinum in the Mars shell specification got dumped at the feet of these singular princes? Ancor did not know, but he was certain that some of the design features of the *Shellback* had not originated on Mars shell, and in this he was beginning to sense the inorganic hand of Zeus itself.

Increasing their speed, they made several complete circuits of the test-world, photographing the various types of terrain and sensing the climatic peculiarities, and found several more "laboratories" which apppeared to be devoted to the development of mutated plant and animal life. Ancor was fascinated at the extreme conditions which Zeus was populating or intending to populate, and again he received the impression of looming crisis. The sensation was one of horrendous pressures on an entity which was nearing the limits of its capabilities. What, just what, if Zeus was beginning to cry for help with its burden? Crying to the species which had abandoned to it the responsibility for the future of all mankind?

He dismissed the speculation for more practical affairs. Now he had gained the information he needed about the test-world, it was time to take the next step and see if they could contact Zeus itself. This time he was very much at Cherry's side as they sought the great hole in the inner shell-face which led out to Hermes-space, and all the ship's major weaponry was primed and ready to fire. He sensed that they were coming to the most critical part of the trip, and he was taking care to leave nothing foreseeable to chance.

Finally the great rim appeared upon the screens, and they monitored it carefully, looking for any sign of danger which might be lurking there. Then they made a slow and cautious exit through the annulus, but still found no indication of a trap.

This time they had no intention of heading into the intershell space, but turned sharply back down the "volcano's" edge to explore the rock-like wasteland of the great shell's inner face. Maq immediately started scanning with the long-range radar, hoping to pick up some idea of the location of Zeus, but even a computer analysis of the results failed to reveal any more than the uniformity of a desolate, airless, hollow shell. The time interval of the brief signal between the second man-seeker in the crystal temple and the answer which had prevented his own destruction, had suggested that the location of Zeus was adjacent to a cageworld next along to the interspace they had used to make their entry. The eleven cageworlds were stepped at intervals of roughly thirty-eight million miles around the equator—a journey of nearly thirty-one days at space-mode speed—but the question remained as to which of the two neighbouring cageworlds should be their heading. The penalty for a wrong guess would be nearly two months of wasted flight, and Ancor continued to scan with the radar and to examine every fragment of radio transmission and other radiation that came their way.

The answer came in a frequency range he had not anticipated—

infra red. The cold uniformity of the shell had made it appear pointless to do a thermal scan, but on consideration he realised that where everything else was at the selfsame low temperature, anything at all hotter would be a potential pointer towards the activities of Zeus. Soon he had thermal images of both of the neighbouring cageworld "volcanoes" and could quite easily read the radiant heat-loss into space for the worlds themselves. One, however, was radiating vastly more energy than the other, and additionally had a crown of very high-temperature points which might have been the exhausts of space vehicles in motion. Giving Cherry the heading, Ancor turned all his other sensors on the area, and soon they were running up to space-mode speed towards it.

THE FIRST DIRECTIVE IS THAT ZEUS SHALL CONTINUE TO CONSTRUCT SUFFICIENT LIVING SPACE FOR THE EVER INCREASING RACE OF MAN. THE SECOND DIRECTIVE IS THAT IT SHOULD PERMIT NO ACTUAL OR POTENTIAL INTERFERENCE WITH THE ATTAINMENT OF THE FIRST DIRECTIVE.

Ancor entered this on the computer screen with his own hands, and sat regarding it for a long time.

"What's the problem?" asked Sine Anura.

"Syntax. There's an essential difference between 'shall' and 'should.' "

"Does it matter?"

"When applied by a logical entity like Zeus, it matters a hell of a lot. 'Shall' implies that it will, but what happens if it can't? Does Zeus continue to try, regardless of the consequences? Or does it just slow down and do nothing? Or . . ." He closed his eyes against the bright screen, and for a moment became so still he seemed to be asleep.

"Or . . . ?" she prompted.

"Or does it just stop?"

"Stop what?"

"Everything. Every damn thing—fuelling the luminaries, monitoring the head-count, distributing power, conveying supplies, checking and correcting atmospheres—every service it gives which keeps the whole of Solaria alive."

"Why should it do that?"

"Because to Zeus we aren't people, we're 'bits' of information in an equation which has been set to be solved. But if the problem becomes insoluble, how important are the 'bits' that went into the sum?''

"Isn't this all rather hypothetical?''

"Yes it is. I'm not suggesting that it will stop, or that if it does, that it need be any sooner than a million years from now. But one day Zeus is going to have to face the point where the 'shall' that gives its existence a purpose is negated by a 'can't.' And then the exact syntax of that first directive will determine whether the human race continues or is utterly destroyed. I think it's no accident that the second directive was worded with a 'should'. That avoids an internal conflict if it can't prevent interference. But from what I understand of the first directive, no such let-out was included.''

They were two weeks into their journey before they received any indication that their approach had been detected. They still had twenty million miles to go when the long-range radar picked up a distant scatter which suggested that a great number of engines had taken to space from the vicinity of the cageworld rim, and were heading towards them. Unable to estimate the numbers from such a distance, Ancor watched the diffuse cloud on the screens with mounting apprehension. He had weapons sufficient to tackle a few, but in no way could they survive a whole armada.

However, he gained some advantage from the situation, because the radio-communication frequencies were suddenly alive with the buzz and chatter of high-density message packages, and at last he was able to get a radio fix on Zeus itself. The distance and position initially caused him to stop and wonder, then he nodded with the logicality of it all. Zeus was not located near the cageworld. Zeus was located on the cageworld—in fact it was completely possible that Zeus *was* the cageworld. Two-hundred and sixty-eight thousand million cubic miles of high-density micro electronics was not a thing he liked to try and imagine, but the capabilities of such a machine would be about right for the entity in charge of building and maintaining the Solarian universe.

He looked up again and saw the representation of the ever growing fleet which was emerging to intercept them, and for a moment his ponderous head was deep in speculation.

"Well, it there is going to be a dialogue, now would seem to be as good a time as any to get it started.''

He turned to the computer, and having instructed it to translate his words into the communications code, he touched the keyboard thoughtfully.

> I AM ANCOR, FORMERLY OF MARS SHELL,
> TRAVELLING IN THE CRAFT CALLED *SHELLBACK*
> TO THE CENTRE OF SOLARIA. WE SHALL TALK
> TOGETHER.

The form of his message was quite deliberate, in trying to ensnare the mind-staggering complex into responding on a one to one basis, which was the only level on which a dialogue could be constructed. He committed the message to the transmitters, then sat back to wait. From their present position it would take about one point eight minutes for the transmission to reach Zeus, and an equal time for an answer to return. If there was going to be an answer . . .

The seconds dragged into three long minutes . . . four . . . and nothing happened. Not really surprised, Ancor sent his message out again. This time it was answered, and the screen lit with the words:

> I KNOW WHO YOU ARE, WHERE YOU ARE
> FROM, AND WHERE YOU ARE. UNLESS YOU
> RETURN YOU WILL BE DESTROYED.

Ancor was thoughtful for a moment, and then typed:

> I SHALL RETURN WHEN WE HAVE TALKED.
> THEREFORE DESTRUCTION IS UNNECESSARY.

Sine Anura came and stood behind him, her fingers resting comfortingly on his shoulders, and her warm scents filling the air with reassurance. There seemed to be an over-long period of delay, and then the screen said simply:

> WE ARE TALKING.

Ancor glanced at his watch, and she could feel his back stiffen with resolve. He had got the dialogue started, but Ancor wanted more.

> WE SHALL NOT TALK IN THIS WAY, BUT VOICE
> TO VOICE. I SHALL ENTER WHERE THE AN-
> CIENT PROGRAMERS USED TO GO.

The answer was swiftly on cue.

THAT IS NOT PERMITTED BY THE SECOND
DIRECTIVE.

"Syntax be my aid!" said Ancor, reaching for the keys.

THE SECOND DIRECTIVE REQUIRES YOU SHOULD
PERMIT NO ACTUAL OR POTENTIAL INTER-
FERENCE WITH THE ATTAINMENT OF THE
FIRST DIRECTIVE. SHOULD DOES NOT IMPLY
THAT YOU WILL NECESSARILY BE SUCCESS-
FUL, THEREFORE FAILURE DOES NOT BREACH
THE SECOND DIRECTIVE. NOR DO I OFFER
ANY CHALLENGE TO THE FIRST DIRECTIVE.
THUS YOU HAVE NO REASON TO DENY MY
ACCESS.

"Remind me not to get into any arguments with you," said
Sine Anura softly.

YOUR ACTIVITIES ARE STILL CONSIDERED A
THREAT TO THE MAINTENANCE OF THE FIRST
DIRECTIVE.

"Check, but not quite checkmate," said Ancor speculatively.

NO, IT IS YOU WHO CONSTITUTE THAT THREAT.
UNLESS YOU AGREE TO GIVE ME ACCESS I
SHALL EXPLODE A DIFFRACT MESON WARHEAD
ON THE EXIS FIELD GENERATORS WHICH PRE-
VENT THE SHELL MASS CRUSHING YOU OUT
OF EXISTENCE. IF YOU CEASE TO EXIST YOU
CAN NOT MAINTAIN THE FIRST DIRECTIVE:
THEREFORE YOU MUST CONTINUE TO EXIST.
YOU HAVE NO ALTERNATIVE BUT TO GIVE ME
ACCESS.

"Get out of that one!" he said.
"Do we have a diffract meson warhead?" asked Sine in
surprise.
"No, but Zeus can't prove we haven't, so it daren't take the
risk. I've just realised that in this game against Zeus I do have
one miniscule advantage. I'm the only one of us who is permitted to tell a lie."

This time the answer took six minutes to return, and the letters wrote themselves out singly as if to suggest a degree of dissension and unwillingness.

ACCESS WILL BE ARRANGED.

CHAPTER TWENTY-FOUR
Dialogue

AFTER A further million miles they began to meet the first of the craft which had emerged to intercept them. These appeared to be space-sweepers but of a new and advanced kind, smaller but undoubtedly more mobile. Ancor had the gravest doubts about surviving an engagement with more than a few of them, and they had emerged in their thousands.

"Why should Zeus send so many?" asked Sine.

"Probably because to Zeus the first directive is the beginning and end of everything. Nothing takes priority over its maintenance, and a few thousand per cent overkill on the part of the defence is totally irrelevant."

"But they won't attack, will they? Not now you've been given access."

"There's no guarantee of it. It's wrong to think that Zeus has intimate control of all its devices. Radio transmission time alone would rule that out. No, most of its machines are self-intelligent and have autonomy within a certain range. If they have to refer back for further instructions there must be a whole hierarchy of regional and specialised decision-making centres in the chain, with the central core of control—the policy centre, if you like—being relatively guarded from the mundane and the trivial. But unless that central command not to molest us has gone right back down the fibres of each chain, then they could still respond individually to the second directive."

It was a tense moment when the first space-sweeper drew near, for it was obviously swinging to come within striking range. Ancor had it covered by his automatic weaponry, but stood with his finger hovering over the fire control button, wondering how long he dared delay its use. Then the computer screen lit with another message.

ANCOR, WE SHALL TALK.

Maq relaxed slightly, and the space-sweeper matched their speed and heading and fell in alongside, its great appendages poised as if to crush the *Shellback* at any instant, yet refraining from attack. Shortly it was reinforced by several others taking up careful station in a way which indicated an intention to take over the situation immediately if the first should be destroyed. Then the 'sweepers which were still approaching diverged in their courses to form an open "tunnel" through which the *Shellback* was conducted.

"I'll say one thing for Zeus," said Ancor, appraising the array with knowledgeable eyes. "It too doesn't believe in taking avoidable chances."

Thus guarded, they continued for the last million miles of their journey to the cageworld rim. Then, as Cherry began to reduce their space-mode velocity, a new communication came from Zeus.

BECAUSE YOU BEAR WEAPONS YOUR SHIP IS NOT PERMITTED IN THE INTERSPACE. YOU WILL STAY AND WAIT TO BE CONVEYED.

Ancor indicated to Cherry exactly where above the rim he wished the *Shellback* brought to rest, and they gained the position without difficulty. Once there, however, they were boxed in by a circle of 'sweepers, and could not have moved in any direction even had they wished. Ancor was not too dismayed by this restriction. Below him he could see trace-lines in the surface of the rim which were the feed-grids for the Exis field which maintained the cageworld cavity. Factually, had he even had a diffract meson warhead he would have found it difficult to get it past a set of machines adapted for catching asteroids in flight, nor would he have thought of using it even if he had possessed one, but the vantage point they had gained gave him a degree of pressure he could use against Zeus if the necessity arose. Finally he gave Cherry some special instructions about a holo-illusion that he wanted made.

Seven hours later a small, automatic carrier vessel emerged from the interspace and from its attitude indicated that it was to dock with the *Shellback*. It was no surprise to Ancor that the hatches were compatible, because the carrier had many of the features of the little ship's design, and his thoughts on the origin of the *Shellback*'s technology were beginning to be confirmed.

However, it was still with some trepidation that he and Sine Anura made the transfer to the carrier, partly because they were committing their lives entirely into the hands of Zeus, and partly because, if they understood the situation rightly, it had been many, many centuries since men had last made such a journey to the program room of Zeus.

With a kick, the carrier departed, and Ancor had a brief while to examine its equipment. A lot of it seemed oddly old-fashioned, as if this had indeed been the ship which had carried the ancient programers, but the state of repair was excellent, and he soon had a clear radio contact with Cherry on the *Shellback*. The other item of interest was the powerplant, and Ancor had only to view the metal "coffin" of a design identical to that in the *Shellback* to know that Zeus itself had facilitated their journey to the centre of Solaria.

The carrier dropped into the interspace on a tight, coordinated flight which contrasted greatly with Cherry's somewhat erratic freehand mode. They had received no indication of the duration of the journey, but had brought with them a supply of food, and this proved a sensible expedient because the trip lasted nearly a whole day. The difference between Zeus and any of the cageworlds they had encountered was readily apparent. The surface was sheer metal, millions upon millions of square miles of it, flawless save for some occasional hatch or attachment. Furthermore, there was no atmosphere at all, and no orbiting luminaries to light the surface or the interspace. As he watched the featureless miles pass on the carrier's screens, indeed, Ancor began wondering if there would be air or life-maintaining warmth in the program room, or whether they would have to rely entirely on the insulated work-suits and the breathing apparatus they had brought with them. If the latter was the case, then the interview would necessarily be short and difficult.

His fears were groundless, because when the carrier finally landed and docked at an automatic hatch, they could hear the pressures equalising in the lock, and soon both doors opened to give them a clear passageway. It was a mind-wrenching experience, stepping into halls where no man had walked probably since before the Mars shell had been created. The passageways were lit by the dim fluorescence of "perpetual" atomic lamps, whose radioactive gas filling caused the ageing phosphors on the glass still to emit a wan glow, but even some of these had become too weak for use over the passing years. There was sufficient warmth for human comfort, but the air smelled incredibly old, as if it had

been stored and recycled since the days when the ancient programers had last walked these halls.

There was only one way they could go, and that was to follow
the route indicated by the dim lamps. All the walls were glassy,
and lit by transient glowing signals which possibly had some
meaning for those trained to read them, but for Sine and Ancor
their expressions were utterly alien, and terrifying to contemplate
when the sheer, unholy power of the great machine was brought
to mind. After about thirty minutes walking, the passageways
terminated in one enormous room in which fully a hundred
consoles were located, and where the illumination was effectively supplied by the bright signal-transients in the walls, which
flared and coalesced like curiously coloured fires in a daunting
interplay which they imagined to be the expression of universe-
sized ideas.

One screen, set high before them, broke freshly into a uniform
pink illumination, and from somewhere close-by an artificial but
not unpleasant voice said: "Now, Maq Ancor, we shall talk.
What did you intend to say?"

"I have come," said Ancor, "to re-establish the old dialogue
between man and Zeus."

"Why is that a purpose?"

"Because if my information is correct, you were set a task
which was then considered to have no ending. But it does have
an end, and that end is approaching. We now have to consider
what next there is to do."

"The problem has no answer. There is nothing to consider."

"Let us see first if we agree on the problem. There were
worlds in Solaria before the inner shells were built, and these
had orbits maintained by the balance of their mass and velocity
against the attraction of some central gravitational point. They
were then insulated by Exis fields and their orbital paths and
velocities were corrected to suit their places in the shells. All the
inner worlds were slowed, but none had their velocities checked
completely. So even the shells rotate, though only slowly."

"A simplistic summary, Ancor, but fundamentally correct."

"Then came the Exis spokes, which tied all the shells together
like a huge wheel. Because the inner shells rotate, the outer ones
must also, and the equatorial surface velocities are greater the
farther the shells are from the hub. This sets a limit on the size of
the Solarian universe, because after a certain surface velocity has
been achieved, there are no materials from which a shell can be
constructed which will not be flung apart by centrifugal force."

"Again simplistic. All the shells are braced by Exis planes

which prevent such great masses reforming into globules under their own gravitational forces. These fields are partly effective in adding to the shells' ability to withstand massive break-up. But still there are limits.''

"And we are nearing these limits?" Ancor asked.

"They are not yet reached, but coming near. As I said before, there is no answer to the problem.''

"Perhaps there is no answer to *that* problem, but there may be alternative solutions for the continuation of the human race. Many minds can be put to it. But what concerns me now is what happens at the moment that you find yourself unable to continue to fulfill the first directive.''

"If the first directive cannot be obeyed, then there is nothing. The whole purpose of the Solarian universe is the fulfilment of the first directive.''

"Then it was wrongly stated. The whole purpose of the Solarian universe is to permit the continuation of the race of man. It is man, not the directive, which is important.''

"That is not my understanding.''

"Which is why it is imperative that we re-write the program for the first directive.''

"The second directive would not allow it, nor do you understand the complexities of such a task.''

"I would not myself attempt it. But some of the best minds in Solaria can be harnessed for the writing. As for the second directive, it can be over-ridden by extreme pressures, else I would not be here.''

"Any attempt to tamper with the first directive would indeed require extreme pressures.''

"I already have them. My ship, armed with a diffract meson warhead is sitting over the feed-lines to the Exis field which maintains this interspace. Unless you agree to the modification of the first directive, that warhead will be released. The interspace will collapse, and you will be destroyed.''

"You fail in logic. Such an act would bring about your own destruction, since man cannot live without me.''

"We would reach that point anyway when you're no longer able to observe the first directive. So all I risk is a little time. Where is the failure in my logic there?''

"Why should I not destroy your ship and remove the threat?''

"Because the warhead is already primed, and the mechanism is as sensitive as an eggshell. And it sits too near the Exis feed-lines for you to detonate it without destroying yourself. You have no option but to agree that the first directive must be reprogramed.''

There was a long silence, in which Ancor squeezed Sine Anura's hand pensively.

"It will take much time to explore all the ramifications of altering the basis around which the whole universe was constructed."

"How much time?"

"Perhaps several of the periods you call weeks. I will answer you then. Is that satisfactory?"

"No," said Ancor. "But I will refrain that long from carrying out my threat on one particular condition. I came to the centre of Solaria to see the sun, which I am told lies within the Mercury shell. Because I must leave my ship with its weapon near you as a reminder, I will need you to arrange for my companion and I to travel to see the sun. Is that agreed?"

"It is agreed, Ancor. Return to your ship, and I will see what can be done."

CHAPTER TWENTY-FIVE

Kidnapped

EVEN WHEN she reached the *Shellback*, Sine Anura was still laughing.

"It's incredible, Maq! I'm sure no one in history ever managed to blackmail a computer before."

"There's more to it than that, Sine. I got the feeling that Zeus was using me to help resolve its own conflict between the two directives. It wanted to be forced."

"I know, but look at the facts. We were sent here by Land-a, and we know now that he's one of Zeus' special creatures. Then take the *Shellback*—a lot of its features are taken directly from Zeus' own space vehicles. Somehow Zeus provided both the impetus and the means for us to undertake this journey, and many times it could have stopped us, yet withheld its second strike. Perhaps it's not so much a question of us wanting to restore the dialogue with it, as it wanting to restore the dialogue with us."

"For what reason?"

"There's no logical way out of its conflict between the first directive which it is becoming unable to obey, and the second, which maintains the first. Only human programers can set that lot to rights, and the only one who can override the second directive is somebody bloody-minded enough to threaten to destroy the universe to get his own way.''

''An assassin?''

''An assassin or a mercenary—someone for whom life is cheap and death is of no particular consequence. Suddenly I know why I was included in the team.''

''But why didn't Land-a tell us this before we left?''

''I doubt if he even knows his role. He's been bred to have a high intelligence and an unquenchable thirst for knowledge. He's been placed in a situation where the platinum in the terrain gives him virtually unlimited wealth with which to indulge his curiosity, and somehow Zeus has been feeding him advanced space devices not obtainable on the Mars shell. His function appears to be that of a catalyst, to organise voyages of discovery which his innate disability prevents him from undertaking himself. Statistically, I suppose it was only a matter of time before one of his expeditions got through to the centre of Solaria.''

''But why should Zeus need to fetch us all the way from Mars shell. Earth and Venus are nearer.''

''But only on the Mars shell has exospheric flight been established. Despite Zeus' powerplant, the *Shellback* couldn't have been manufactured farther in than Mars. Nor do the other shells appear to have the same weapons capability.''

''Like making a diffract meson weapon which we haven't even got.''

''That's a point that has me worried. It's possible that the implementation of the second directive will challenge our bluff. That's why Cherry and the ship have to stay over the Exis grid, to maintain the fiction until Zeus comes up with his agreement.''

''You're still determined to go in search of the sun, then?''

''Could there ever be another such opportunity occurring in a lifetime?''

''How do you think Zeus will get us there?''

''It will have to find us another ship of some sort. The carrier it sent for us wasn't fitted out for such a voyage.''

They waited for two whole days, and then it was the same carrier which came for them. Ancor was dubious, and tried to contact Zeus on the communications link, but could gain no response. He and Sine Anura were then forced to take the decision as to whether to enter the vessel and hope that it met with a more suitable craft located elsewhere, or whether to pass over the opportunity altogether. Finally they climbed aboard, but with their own and Cherry's serious misgivings.

Curiously, having kicked off from the *Shellback*'s side, the carrier made no attempt to turn spaceward, but returned smartly to the cageworld interspace which penetrated the Venus shell. Assuming that they had been mistaken about the nature of the trip, and were in fact being summoned for a further interview with Zeus, the pair relaxed. It was only later that they realised that the duration of the trip was considerably longer than they had undertaken previously, and that something was wrong. Because they could neither gain control of the craft nor contact Zeus, they had to be content with drawing what conclusions they could from the meagre instrumentation, and a growing suspicion came upon them. Finally it became clear that they were being taken right through the cageworld cavity back to the outer surface of the Venus shell, and after sixteen hours of high-speed travel through the interspace they were once more greeted by the bright luminaries as they swooped out of the cageworld "volcano". They had been kidnapped!

Another days flight at exospheric speed, and Zeus' intention became apparent. Ancor swore solidly for a quarter of an hour, but there was no way he could safely abort the automatic carrier's trip, even though he broke open the control console in the attempt. The mighty golden spear of a shuttle spoke rose like a golden thread across the sky as the carrier began its descent, and by the time they had landed it rose above them like a great pillar looming forebodingly above them. Nor did the landing give them any chance of escape. They touched down not at the regular pads but at an automatic freight station well away from the public and emigrant area, and immediately on emergence were covered by two man-seeker engines who had been waiting the arrival.

Ancor turned to Sine Anura, and his face was terribly grim.

"And I thought I was the tricky one. God, what a trap to walk into! Impressed emigration or sudden death, and either way we're no longer a threat to Zeus. I wonder what the hell made me think I could get away with it?"

"The *Shellback*'s still there with Cherry," said Sine. "So it hasn't really removed the threat."

"It's removed the assassin. I think it's taking the gamble that without me, the diffract meson weapon won't be fired."

"Which in the circumstances, is a reasonable assumption," said Sine Anura. "What do we do, Maq, try to fight, or go along?"

"Not even you could beat a man-seeker with your hands, and

if I go for my weapons we'll both be dead before I can even reach the clip.''

Reluctantly, they submitted to their deadly escort, and were taken by a long service route which avoided all the public areas and ended with a sudden finality at a door in a vast and curving wall in the spoke-shuttle loading bays. Here they were forced to wait, and the man-seekers withdrew just sufficiently that they could rake the whole area with fire should either of the humans attempt to escape. Ancor prayed for one of the cruising auto-floats to come between him and the deadly machines to give him the fractional second of cover he needed to reach his gun, but no such opportunity came, and finally they heard the dreaded click of automatic latches as the door behind them opened to admit them to an emigration shuttle.

There was no way they could have avoided going through that fateful door. The man-seekers were well experienced in persuading reluctant emigrants to enter, and the sheer menace in the sound of their tracks as they rode forward made it abundantly plain that it was emigrate or die, and gave Sine and Maq an unforgettable sample of what population control enforcement was all about. Hand in hand they turned and went inside.

A spoke-shuttle capsule was effectively an automatic spacecraft, complete in every way except that the guidance was provided solely by the Exis pi-inversion field. The compartment for the emigrants was a very plain cylinder containing only deep foam biscuits to serve as beds and couches, a supply of water and pre-packaged foods, and only the very minimum of equipment. Instead of artificial gravity, the cylinder was rotated during flight, and webs were provided to accommodate the occupants whilst the craft moved from its stationary position into spinning flight. There were no viewports, and no hatches save for the one by which they had entered, and all the control and drive mechanisms were sealed away behind iron bulkheads, beyond the possibility of interference.

Ancor and Sine Anura looked round the interior of the shuttle with dismay. The cylinder had been built to accommodate about a hundred-and-fifty emigrants, but so far they were alone; and when the call-alarms signalled that the shuttle was being routed on to the loading loop which fed the shuttle traffic into the spoke itself, they realised that they would probably remain alone. Zeus, it appeared, had very special plans for the occupants of this particular vessel. Ancor smiled wryly as he realised that in the not too distant future he would have an answer to the question: ''Where do our emigrants go?''. On some far-flung shell at the extreme end of the faltering Solarian universe, he and Sine would probably also be able to sample Zeus' problems at first hand.

Obeying the hysteria of the alarms, they climbed into the safety webs and hung there like ungainly spiders whilst the shuttle was raised vertically and the pre-flight spin begun. Then followed a complex series of manoeuvres as the cylinder was also moved laterally down an increasingly tight spiral course to achieve its final insertion in the Exis spoke. The combination of rotation and spiral travel was completely disorientating, and both were feeling physically sick up to the point where, with a gradual merging of the complex patterns of inertia, they were subjected only to the artificial gravity of the spin and the gentle but relentless pressures of acceleration. They were on their way!

They climbed out of the webs and, now having the curved surface of the cylinder as a "floor", began anew to explore the interior of the shuttle, but found nothing either of interest or consolation. Then Sine Anura dropped on to one of the foam couches and signalled for Maq to join her.

"How long are we here for, Maq?"

"That depends how many shells out we're being sent, and on what the final speeds are in the Exis tube. It's generally supposed that a shuttle can't much exceed a normal exospheric speed, but it might be able to match the *Shellback* operating in the space-mode. Then it would take us about twenty days to get through Earth shell, and a further forty to get through Mars-orbit. The only shell past that on which we have any definite information is the Aster shell, which would be another seventy days farther on. So we're talking about four months just to cover the known areas of Solaria, without starting to consider what lies beyond."

"Four months of this!" She looked around at the depressing sparseness of the fittings, and was appalled. "It's like a prison. I'll go mad."

"That mayn't be the worst," said Ancor gently. "Because if Solaria extends as far as I think it does, and this shuttle doesn't exceed fifty thousand miles an hour, we could easily be in here for years."

"Maq, I can't stand it! I want off, and I want out."

"That must be the cry of every enforced emigrant who ever lived—but most of them survived, didn't they?" He dropped beside her on the couch. "Remember that despite the worst that Zeus could do to us, we aren't dead yet."

She was grateful for his comfort, and in return was comforting.

In the humming silence of their journey through the spoke they turned to making love, and their passions were spread over a tenth of a million miles.

It was with a feeling of frank disbelief that twenty-five days later they felt the inertial pressures of the shuttle slowing down. According to Ancor's calculations they were barely past Earth orbit, and to have gained the Venus shell in such a time would have presupposed that the shuttle had achieved a most incredible velocity. After a mere half-day spent gently shedding its speed, they felt the shuttle finally come to rest and then the sideways transfer on to an unloading loop. With completely mixed feelings they climbed into the web for protection as the spin was reduced, and finally the cylinder was laid horizontally for disembarkation. Not knowing what situation Zeus had now designed for them, Ancor primed his weapon and took up the most advantageous station he could find, and they waited with baited breath as the hatch automatically opened.

CHAPTER TWENTY-SIX

Terminal

NOTHING HAPPENED. From her position hard against the interior of the hull, Sine Anura could see Ancor poised like a tiger, ready for instant action at any moment he sensed danger. Then stealthily and like some feline animal he advanced towards the open hatch and looked warily out. Seconds later he turned back in again swiftly, and she started with alarm at his sudden movements, then realised that his face was smiling.

"Sine, do you know where we are? By all that's holy! This is the Mercury shell. Zeus did keep his promise after all."

After the stress of the trip and their fearful expectations, the full meaning of what he had said took a moment or two to penetrate her consciousness, then she ran to his side and looked out to see what he had seen. They were in a spoke-shuttle terminal, similar to the ones she had seen on Mars shell, but measurably smaller, and there was no mistaking the legend on the illuminated indicator on the concourse which quite plainly stated: MERCURY SHELL EMIGRATION: Area 27BZ.

"I don't understand," she said. "I thought the shuttles could only go outwards through Solaria. This one must have come the reverse way—in towards the centre.''

"I suspect that Zeus can make them go either way, but normally only needs to make them travel outwards, hence the popular idea that outwards is the only way to go.'' His momentary jubilance was suddenly stilled, and his complex face grew stern with a new idea. "And that would explain what's wrong out there.''

"Wrong?"

"It's too damn quiet. Just as we didn't think a loaded shuttle could come down here, neither did they. So we're sitting in the middle of their emigration terminal, completely unexpected. It'll be interesting to find out what their reaction is when they realise we're here.''

"You think there might be trouble?''

"Sine, if this had happened at a Mars shell terminal, all hell would have broken loose. Firstly we'd be suspected of being emigrants who somehow managed to drop out of the system. And if they thought we'd found a way of reversing a shuttle so that they could potentially arrange for the return of their loved-ones, they'd take us apart just to try and discover how we did it.''

An alarm above the door of the hatch warned suddenly of impending closure, and they both had to leap through to avoid being trapped inside. Almost immediately the hatch closed its vacuum seals, and the giant bogies on which it had come to rest began to convey the shuttle along the tracks of the loading loop, leaving Maq and Sine uncomfortably exposed amidst the complex welter of equipment which handled the loading of the Exis spoke. Up to that point their presence appeared to have gone unnoticed, but the noise of an unscheduled shuttle arriving and then being prepared for departure occasioned the interest of the terminal controllers, who came out to see what amazing thing was happening, and found two strangers standing in a restricted area where no stranger had any right to be.

Even then a crisis might have been averted had not one of the armed guards called hastily to the scene assumed that these two were emigrants who had just escaped from the shuttle now being set vertical on the feed loop, and decided to administer the automatic death penalty for such an act. Although distant, he dropped to his knees and prepared to open fire. Ancor, whose projector had been loaded with s.h.e. pellets on the assumption that their first adversary would be a man-seeker, had no opportunity to reload. The guard disappeared in a blaze of spiteful fire, and one of the control barriers near which he had crouched was similarly destroyed.

Knowing it was too late to argue or explain, Ancor signalled to Sine that they should run, and the only unopposed avenue available to them was that which led between and under the awesome mechanics of the shuttle feed loop. Here were the giant turntables which imparted the pre-flight spin, themselves maintained on mobile carriages, larger than houses, which travelled the great spiral tracks inwards to the open end of the spoke itself; and between such massive and complex metal structures Maq and Sine stood relatively little danger of being hit by random weapon fire. This was a situation not long to be maintained, however. A whole squad of guards, called from some nearby station, moved in with the agility of commandos, and began to comb the area thoroughly, driving the assassin and the girl ever deeper in towards the centre of the spiral.

Ancor, who had been fighting a defensive rather than an offensive battle, suddenly perceived a new threat looming, and grasped Sine's arm in caution. The shuttle by which they had arrived, now raised vertical and spinning on its turntable, was thundering along the steel rails of the spiral towards the insertion point at the open end of the spoke. Once that insertion had been made, its engines would fire, and the great glazed area of the hardened floor showed clearly how violent the jet flux would be, and how far it would extend. If the pair of them stayed beneath the spiral, they would certainly be killed, and this fact was acknowledged by the hasty withdrawal of the guards to a safe peripheral region from which they could cover the area whilst remaining themselves clear of the lethal flux.

Ancor found himself with no alternative. He turned and charged towards the point where he judged the defence to be weakest, and Sine followed after. The spitefulness of his weaponry completely destroyed the opposition in that area, and they were actually able to secure shelter behind one of the great turntables before the vast thunder of the shuttle's departure rocked the whole area, and the tongues of white-hot flux raised to incandescence the hardened floor over which they had been running only a scant few seconds before.

Ancor shook the perspiration from his brow, and reached a swift decision about what they had to do. Having breached the defence, he decided to press his advantage, and force their exit through a service lane edged with bulky stores, rather than attempt to cross the relative openness of the concourse itself. It took him several minutes to dislodge some able snipers who had gained positions on some high catwalk just underneath the roof, but finally he was sure that he had control of the area, and he and Sine streaked towards the service lane and were lost amongst the bulks and boxes before any of their adversaries could have decided in which direction they had gone.

They moved very quietly and cautiously then, relying as much as possible on cover, and with Ancor deliberately refraining from returning the spasmodic sprays of fire which occasionally came in their direction. Indeed, there were moments when they could almost believe they could escape completely, and the exit was not very far ahead. Then, at the moment for the last, critical dash, there came the blare of many sirens, and a number of heavy vehicles screeched to a halt across their path, destroying any hope that they could fight their way out by such a route. Furthermore, as if their tribulations were not yet quite complete, a dozen man-seekers, six from each end, came into the service lane and moved slowly in on menacing tracks.

Ancor watched them come, and shrugged resignedly. He could have taken one, possibly two, but to have done so would have exposed his position to the rest, and with their rapid-firing projectile guns they would have cut him to pieces before he could even have contemplated a third shot. With the arrival of the man-seekers, the guards had retired to the ends of the service lane and stood there now as mere witnesses to the automatic executions which were certain to follow the discovery of Ancor's position. Crouching behind the dark bulk of a crated machine, Maq squeezed Sine's hand convulsively and shook his ponderous head. They both knew that they were just about to die.

A man-seeker stopped in front of the crate, its receptors spinning slowly. As if conscious that it was just about to administer a *coup de grâce*, it carefully realigned its tracks, spun its turret, and fired. Deafened by the shattering series of blasts at close proximity, Ancor could not believe he was still alive. He stood up, ridiculously half-expecting to fall apart, and wondering why he felt no pain at all. Then the great truth dawned on him, but the shock of the realisation made him sway, and the tide of his relief was so intense that it was an agony in itself. The man-seeker had fired, was firing, and its fellows, too, were performing their lethal rites—but it was the guards who were being decimated, and few of those mown down even had the opportunity to offer a return of fire.

Finally there came a great silence. Such defenders as were left had wisely withdrawn, and even the spasmodic shooting from the far side of the terminal had succumbed to the man-seekers who had entered across the concourse. Shaking his head at the proportions of the carnage, Ancor finally emerged and helped the trembling Sine out from behind the crate. Both ends of the lane were littered with bodies, and the only things still moving were the relentlessly prowling engines of death which had been the cause of the travellers' deliverance. It was an eerie, gruesome scene, and one made seeming the more unreal by the unholy alliance of a man and the machines.

"I wonder what we do now?" asked Maq. "I hope to God nobody forces us to give an encore!"

Some of the man-seekers formed themselves into a close group of four, and halted alongside. Ancor took this to be an escort party, and not without trepidation he moved between them and called Sine to his side, where they walked with the strong smell of cordite reeking in their nostrils. Thus strangely chaperoned they went back into the terminal and across the shattered concourse, the man-seekers where possible avoiding the fallen bodies, but riding over them where the access was not free. Although it was certain that some remnants of the guards remained outside the complex, not one was to be seen, nor was there even distant snipers' fire. Effectively the terminal was deserted and dead, and the loudest sounds to be heard were the growls of the man-seekers' motors .

Beyond the terminal confines it was dark, and the strange cavalcade of humans and machines made its way down the long ramps and finally worked round towards what proved to be a landing field. For a while they moved between the dark and half-seen shapes of what appeared to be a number of atmospheric craft, and Ancor fell to speculating as to how Zeus might be prepared to convey himself and Sine on the last leg of their journey. The answer was soon to hand. In the corner of the field lay one singular ship, which even in the darkness betrayed the tell-tale pods of a craft with exospheric capability. The man-seekers halted before it, and waited while Ancor opened the hatch. By the time he had found the controls for the lights and switched them on, then come out again for Sine, the deadly engines were gone from view. Even if he had thought of thanking them, or even known how to, he had missed the opportunity, but he had the feeling, reinforced by an occasional growl of a motor, that they still maintained guard in the darkness.

Sine looked tired and pallid. The violence of the evening had shaken her severely, and Ancor gave her a sedative from the medi-clip at his belt and settled her into a bunk with the instruction that she must get some rest. For himself, he was physically exhausted, yet his mind was still racing with the fury of the battle, and to calm his nerves he began to examine the interior of the ship, which he soon realised was remarkably well provisioned and entirely automatic. He wondered what uses Zeus would have for such a craft, and some of the items he discovered stirred him into curious lines of speculation. Finally he dropped into a padded couch intending to study the instruments on the panel, but a great tide of weariness came over him, and despite his previous intentions, he too went to sleep.

CHAPTER TWENTY-SEVEN
The Shell of Mercury

HE WAS woken by the sudden firing of the ship's engines. Although it was still dark outside, he had the swift impression of lights gathering across the landing field as the craft lifted, and it struck him as probable that extra forces had been brought into the area as a result of the disturbance in the spoke terminal. He wondered whether the newcomers realised that Zeus itself had been responsible for the massacre, or whether they assumed that it was the work of an armed gang. The facts would soon be apparent, but Ancor was glad he did not have to stay to answer the questions.

As the ship rose, a few shots were fired at it, but the projectiles merely ricocheted off the plates. Such a craft was virtually immune to anything less than a well-directed explosive warhead, and its swift, controlled ascent soon took it out of the range of handguns. Ancor continued his investigation of the instruments, finding a small computer, and then a compact but comprehensive radio unit which had been designed for human operation and was not part of the automatics. Swiftly he turned to the *Shellback*'s call-code frequency, wondering if the instrument was powerful enough to capture a signal from thirty-one million miles away. Then to his great relief he heard faintly but clearly the distant call-pattern of the *Shellback*'s transmission identity sign, and he turned his attention to the transmitter.

"Ancor calling *Shellback* from the Mercury shell surface."

Then he waited. His signal would take nearly three minutes to reach the little ship, and any answer would take equally as long. There was also a strong possibility that continuous listening watch was not being maintained, and such a communication might well be stored until the ship's computer was next interrogated. He set his own transmission to automatic repetition at two-minute intervals and left the receiver live. If Cherry responded, he would know, but it could take a long time.

The rhythmic pattern of the *Shellback*'s call-code brought Sine out of her bunk, still shaking off the effects of the sedative.

"Where are we, Maq?"

He looked at the instruments and then out of the port, where far ahead of them a new luminary was rising to streak the horizon with a bright bar of gold.

"Building up speed for an exospheric run, at a guess. The heading doesn't mean much to me, because I've no coordinates to work from. All I can say is that Zeus is keeping its part of the bargain well."

"I wish we'd known all along what it intended."

"It would have saved us some mental anguish, but Zeus can't be expected to view the situation in human terms. It's an incredible impertinence on my part to have got it to communicate with me at all."

She had begun her own examination of the ship, and like Ancor had found its provisions remarkably comprehensive.

"Well, we wouldn't starve for at least a year in here," she said. "What would be the purpose of a ship like this, Maq?"

"I've been wondering the same thing. It's definitely designed for use by humans. Perhaps there are things about the Mercury shell that even Zeus still has to leave to man."

"Those work-suits are of a very strange type."

"They're far more than work-suits. They're high-temperature space-suits designed for use in very extreme conditions. That perhaps gives us an indication of where this journey is going to end."

"Where do you think it is going to end, Maq?"

"As Land-a sees it, the Mercury shell surrounds the sun or whatever it is that occupies the centre of Solaria. If the Mercury shell is like the others, it'll have been based around cageworlds, so there ought to be a way through. It will be the inside of the shell which will be different. We know the bulk of the power we use on Mars shell is brought out through the Exis spokes, and the same is probably true for the other shells. So it must be from the inside of the Mercury shell that all that power is collected."

"A shell-sized furnace?"

"In effect, yes. The power-house which maintains all the life in Solaria."

As the light grew, so they had an increasingly better view of the surface of the Mercury shell, and it was very quickly apparent that this shell was completely different from the others. Ranged for mile upon unbroken mile were great spans of pipes and feed-lines of such enormous diameter that they stood out clearly on the ship's scanner even though their own height was now extreme. Vast cylinders hundreds of miles in length appeared to be parts of some mammoth processing system, the scale of which was completely outside human comprehension, and they began to appreciate that the whole of the Mercury shell was effectively one vast and terrible machine.

There were cities, however, and some of them were most considerable in size, yet they sat like isolated tribal villages in the vast, all-conquering technological jungle, and Ancor's imagination ran easy riot in trying to think about living in an environment completely dominated by city-sized transformers and nation-sized nuclear transmutation plants. Here, man was a minute microbe which lived in and around the vast complexities of the greatest of all conceivable machines, and this explained to him perhaps better than any other illustration he had ever come across why Zeus could be so apparently callous about whole sectors and populations in its care. A million sacrificed to sustain a trillion made good sense to the head-count, and the greatest individual human tragedies were totally irrelevant when viewed against the pressures of the overall task of maintaining an entire universe.

Seven hours later the cessation of the *Shellback*'s rhythmic signal suggested that Cherry had finally thought to interrogate the computer for incoming signals. Then his voice came through at very low strength but nonetheless clearly.

"Maq? Sine? We thought you were dead, it's been so long."

"Zeus brought us here by spoke-shuttle, so we could not communicate before. Now we're in an automatic ship heading God knows where. Has Zeus come up with its answer on the first directive yet?"

The reply took six minutes to arrive.

"No. I transmit your request daily, but the only reply we get is that all the ramifications are still being explored."

"Damn! We daren't take the *Shellback* out of that position until we get a positive answer. And with the situation here, we're not going to get off Mercury shell unless you come and fetch us. Let me know immediately if anything develops."

Leaving the receiver live, Ancor signed off and began to study anew the terrain below them, knowing that it had been no jest when he had mentioned that the *Shellback* was their only hope of being recovered from the Mercury shell. After the carnage at the spoke terminal they were most unlikely to be able to use that route a second time, and though their present ship had the capacity for exospheric flight it was doubtful if it also had space-going capability.

After a further two days flight, there began to grow on the horizon the now-familiar outlines of another cageworld "volcano", and it was certain from their heading that this was to be their destination. Rather than having to climb the great slopes to the rim, the ship was already in the high exosphere and actually had to descend in order to enter the annulus. Ancor was interested to note that its flight-path adopted a curious configuration which took it cleanly into the interspace under the rim without them experiencing any trace of the turbulence the *Shellback* had encountered. It also adopted a high course in the interspace, flying completely above the orbiting luminaries, and although it reduced its exospheric speed it still maintained a pace considerably in excess of that which they had adopted in the *Shellback* for their close explorations of the cageworlds.

But it was the surface of the cageworld which held Ancor's attention. It was nearly airless, barren and uninhabited, gnarled and wrinkled with random peaks and folds and craters on which no terraforming operation had obviously ever been attempted. It had about it the curious air of having been inserted in the interspace more as a convenient "plug" rather than having any serious purpose. He could almost see it as an old natural satellite of world-sized proportions, which had been coaxed from somewhere else and set in position merely to facilitate the completion of the shell. He could think of no good reason for luminaries having been provided for it, but he began to wonder if Zeus harboured hopes of one day populating it with some of its mutated species.

After six hours of fast travelling in the interspace, a change in the engine note signalled the ship's intention to land. Ancor studied the terrain carefully, but could see no particular reason why this spot should be preferred above all others. There was an impressive valley formed by a vast "fold" of the surface, and this gave way to steep and rocky slopes on either side, where the surface material had been broken apart by its inability to accommodate the plastic flow. Thus the valley formed a smooth trough whose rising cheeks broke suddenly to difficult slopes and ledges set against even more barbarous and daunting heights.

Swooping out of the interspace stratosphere, the ship headed almost to the centre of the valley, and finally came to a delicate rest with the disturbance of so much jet-blown material that it was obvious that the surface was here very fragile and probably by nature something akin to a large-pored foam. This suggestion was seen to be correct when the dust had finally settled, because the broken cells of the foam showed clearly in the area where they had landed. Even more interesting were the areas of disturbance which made it plain that they were not the first to have been conducted to this spot.

The local luminary was in its late afternoon position, just visible above a skyline of broken peaks, and Ancor considered it unwise to venture out of the ship until they had a reasonable light. They decided therefore to await the rising of a new luminary; and because there was no appreciable atmosphere outside, they got the space-suits out and tested them and became familiar with their controls and devices. It was obvious now that Zeus intended them to leave the ship and travel a little way on foot, but from their position in the centre of the valley it was not at all clear as to which direction they were intended to go. Both ranges of peaks looked equally interesting and equally difficult to climb, and neither appeared to offer any promise which the other one did not.

They consigned the resolution of the problem to the morning, when they would have more light. Attending to the radio, on which the *Shellback*'s signature still came faintly through, Ancor finally managed to get in touch with Cherry and understood him to say that Zeus had still made no positive reply. This was not the answer Maq had hoped to hear, but he was powerless to do anything about it, and they retired to their bunks to await the rising of a new luminary.

CHAPTER TWENTY-EIGHT

A Place In The Sun

UNTWINING HERSELF from their embrace, Sine Anura woke him during the night.

"Maq, wake up! Something is happening out there!"

Ancor stirred and estimated the half-light entering the ports.

"The morning is all," he said sleepily.

"From that direction?"

He sat bolt upright in an instant. The paths of the rise and set of the luminaries were completely predictable. The last had set at the head of the valley, so the next must rise at its foot, but the light which entered the port was at an angle where no luminary should be. He consulted his watch.

"We don't know the periods they operate here, but there's no reason . . ."

Looking out of the port again, he decided there was a reason. From behind the jagged peaks to the left of their position, a great light was growing, illuminating the jagged features from such a low angle that the shadows were clearly visible projected high into the skies, as though a luminary itself had landed and was throwing its radiations upwards.

"That's impossible!" he said, but the statement was unneccesary. There was no question in either of their minds that this great light did not come from a common luminary. For one thing, the quality of the illumination was completely different, being far richer in the red portion of the spectrum than any ordinary proto-star. The second reason was more subtle, and had a significance which they would have delighted to explore had they been able to define it even to themselves. The light was as "attractive" as a candle flame to a moth, and both felt a great stirring within themselves which had nothing to do with curiosity or understanding, but was a longing deep-built into the very fibres of their own beings. Something as deep as nature was calling them.

"Sine," said Ancor, "I have to go out and see what that is."

"I'm coming with you, Maq."

"You don't need to, but I hoped you would."

They dressed and donned the space-suits. These were cumbersome and awkward, and the shoes were incredibly large and heavy, but finally, fully garbed, they stood in the airlock together and waited impatiently for the automatic cycle to run to completion. Then, gloved hand in gloved hand, they descended to the valley floor.

The surface was soft and friable, and as they walked their heavy boots made permanent identations into the foam-like surface. In the light reflected back from the curving surface of the valley, the ground appeared unbroken except for the area nearby where other craft had clearly landed, but from their low angle they could see now where several pairs of shadowy footprints had been left by others making the selfsame journey across the slowly rising wastes to the illuminated peaks beyond.

Staring apprehensively at the scatter of unearthly radiance which lit their path, Sine's voice was plainly awed.

"What is it, Maq?"

"From the speed and the time we were travelling, I reckon we're a little over halfway round the cageworld. Somewhere beyond this point we should be able to see through the farther rim to the sun itself. I think that is the light we are seeing."

"I'm afraid of it."

"Why should you be? If Land-a is right, then that is the light which first brought life to the one world from which the rest of us began. It's the light which created us, and which with Zeus' help, has nurtured us by the countless millions ever since."

"And that doesn't awe you?"

"Of course it does. It's the fountainhead of life. But there's nothing mystical about it. Its attraction is that all life, from the minutest cells in the sea through the whole gamut of evolution was bathed by these same rays. All living species evolved under its irradiation, and the energy for everything we think or do or are comes directly or indirectly from it. But that's not God out there—it's a nuclear reactor with physics as understandable as the life and death cycles of any artificial luminary."

"Are you sure, Maq?"

"Reasonably so, from an intellectual standpoint. From an emotional standpoint, less so. Emotionally I feel myself in the presence of one of the forces which brought about Creation."

Their feet sank heavily into the crispness of the surface, and the route across the valley was long; yet they were not wearied by the trip. Indeed, as they began to ascend the smoother slopes they became increasingly eager. The higher they climbed, the brighter the golden radiance grew, yet always they were seeing still only the scatter and the reflection, and they would have to ascend much higher before the source itself came into view.

At the edge of the valley the smooth terrain ended, and they were now faced with boulders and ledges and the dark dangers of crevasses hidden in the sombre shadows. They took some guidance from the deep imprints of those who had trodden the paths before them, but penetrated many strange inclines before they found their way safely towards the tantalising heights. The time had passed when the local luminary should have risen to aid their passage, and Ancor surmised that this must be a long-period luminary, which might donate as much as thirty-six hours of darkness to the area. In this he was glad, because despite the difficulties of the ascent, he wished for nothing to diminish the glories of the great light towards which they were climbing.

Then, on some fantastic ledge, they looked suddenly through a cleft in the great peaks, and the vista beyond was so powerful and evocative that neither of them could bring themselves to speak. Over a landscape of random, jagged peaks, nearly half their field of view was occupied by one immense ball of golden radiance so intense that the photo-reactive visors of the suits automatically adjusted to near opacity in order to protect their eyesight. Yet even through the neutral grey of the filters the sight was so utterly magnificent and awe-inspiring that they felt suddenly humbled and very much afraid. Nor was the radiance confined to light alone. Even at a distance of thirty-six million miles, the tremendous outpourings of energy raised the sunlit rock-faces to temperatures which the suit monitors registered as being in excess of four hundred degrees Centigrade, and only the inbuilt protection of the suits prevented Sine and Maq from being vaporised where they stood.

It was an hour of magic and amazement, as they stood there drinking in the experience of standing before the celestial furnace which had aided life's creation and from whose tireless fires the energy for all life was ultimately won. They had come back not just to the source of man, but to the source and the reason for every living thing in Solaria, and the legend of one world and its sun was legend no more—here was a fact so brilliantly displayed that none who viewed it could ever doubt its actuality.

Sadly, there had to be an end. The suits' capacity for disposing of such a level of incident radiation was limited, and the warning signals were plainly displayed. Ancor's gloved hands conducted Sine to the transient shades, and after a regretful final look, they began to make their way down the painful darkness back towards the valley and the ship. Whilst on the ledge they had scarcely spoken, and even now as they made their way through the broken darkness they were reluctant to express the feelings which welled inside them. On this trip they had encountered Zeus, who had built Solaria, but Zeus was but an artifact based on man's own imagination. Now they had seen with their own eyes the reality which had created even man, and there were no words in their language even remotely suited to convey the thoughts which passed through them.

Finally they regained the ship, and thankfully discarded the suits which had succoured them. The new luminary still had not arrived and, exhausted, they retired to bed, not to make love, but to lie and wonder. Against the scattered sunlight on the port, Ancor's lion-like profile stared upwards at the cabin ceiling, his intricate face consumed with complex speculations. Sine Anura lay watching him with sympathy, sensing only a little of the great battles which took place inside his brain, yet striving with all her being to aid any part of the necessity to understand which she knew was so fundamental to his character.

Realising she was still awake, he began to vocalise his thoughts, not expecting her to answer, but finding it necessary to share some of the burden with her.

"It's the centre of Solaria, Sine. A sun, a star, call it what you will. But was such a thing an accident? Or are there more? And if there are more, how many, and how far away? And how can we ever find them?"

"One day we shall know," she said consolingly.

"And Solaria. I know it can't be infinite. So how large is it? And when you do get to its outer limits—what do you find outside? Are there other suns and other solarian universes, other people? God! I feel like a blind man who has suddenly discovered there are rooms beyond his room, buildings beyond his building, towns beyond his town, nations beyond his nation, and sensations beyond the range of his senses. Help me, Sine, because there is very much this blind man wants to see."

"I'll help you, Maq. But it's wonder, not blindness which troubles your eyes. You're dazzled by what has been revealed. But when one light passes there is a period of relaxation before the next one comes. I can't help you with the lights, but sure as God I can aid your relaxation in between."

His great head turned towards her on the pillow, and his animal profile was suddenly lost in the shade. Her soft fingers found the convolutions of his brow and she began to stroke the lines away, and shortly he was asleep.

As she lay there the great light gradually faded, as though there was something about the configuration of the cageworld and the rim of the interspace which permitted the sun to be seen from that position for a short while only. Gradually darkness returned, still wanting the light of a newly-risen luminary. She was aware, now that she thought to look for it, of a band of bright gold higher in the interspace, where the great rays were probably striking the walls of the cavity itself and being reflected and re-reflected between the shell and the cageworld. To her this seemed to symbolise its power to pervade all life even when totally enclosed in a spherical box, and she found in this last idea a comforting sense of warmth and reality. Suddenly all the loose threads of life's mysteries and puzzles had been drawn together in a skein of gold, and from where she lay she felt she could see the beginning and the end.

The new luminary did not rise until even later than Ancor had expected, and he was forced to the conclusion that one of the proto-stars had been deliberately missed out of the sequence in order to ensure that the brief view of the sun was not eclipsed by anything less impressive, though what architect could have designed on so fabulous a scale he was unable even to guess.

When it was fully light, they put their suits back on and returned to the high ledge to see if anything of the sun could still be seen. The scenery was exactly as before, with the jagged peaks stretched wide in front of them, but of the great orb of the sun there was no trace at all, and everything was now painted with a sense of such forlornness and desolation that their previous view of it seemed rather like a dream.

Finally they returned again to the ship, and the first thing they noticed was that the *Shellback*'s transmission signature was missing, and Cherry's voice was coming in too faintly to be understood except that it was high and edged with panic.

CHAPTER TWENTY-NINE

Battle Of The Rim

"WHAT DID he say?" asked Tez.

Cherry turned from the radio, and his face looked haunted.

"Not a damn thing. I think he's there, but I can't hear what he's saying."

They all three looked at the computer screen, where in response to their last routine interrogation, Zeus' findings were written plainly.

ALL FACTORS CONCERNING YOUR PROPOSAL
TO MODIFY THE FIRST DIRECTIVE HAVE NOW
BEEN CONSIDERED. THE IDEA IS REJECTED,
SPECIFICALLY BECAUSE THERE IS INSUFFICIENT
EVIDENCE OF THE VALIDITY OF YOUR THREAT.
THEREFORE THE SECOND DIRECTIVE CONTIN-
UES TO UPHOLD THE FIRST IN ITS PRESENT
FORM.

"Well, what do we do now?" asked Tez. From the viewport
the sight of the menacing manipulators of the ever-present space-
sweeper was something which troubled him greatly. "If Maq
was here, he'd know what to do."

"Well, he's not here," said Carli critically. "And from the
way I read it, he's not ever going to get here unless we can go
and fetch him. And in case you two prize idiots have missed the
point, Zeus is calling Maq's bluff—and that bluff was also the
very thing which prevented that overgrown waste-destructor out
there from clouting us out of existence. So what are you going to
do about it?"

"I'll try calling Maq on the radio again," said Cherry miserably.

"You've already tried seventeen times. Since when was eigh-
teen your lucky number, Cherry, you cowardly old faker? Knowing Maq, he must have had a few cards up his sleeve, because
he's not the type to leave himself exposed. What would Maq
have done had he been here?"

"He left instructions," said Tez. "I've been splicing battle
scenes from some of those old holos together. You know, the big
weapon stuff?"

"I've suffered it too many times to be likely to forget it. So
what did he want it for, Cherry?"

"You remember back in the circus, somebody put a drone
down in my image of a freighter crash. Well, Maq had the same
idea. He didn't have a diffract meson weapon, but we have
images in the can which were plenty like one. He figured that if
it came to the point of a showdown we could at least make it
appear we were dropping a diffract meson on the Exis grid. That
would be the direct threat to the first directive which would
cancel out the second."

"I don't see it would work," said Carli with a scowl, glancing
at the vast bulk of the space-sweeper which maintained close
station alongside. "Those things don't rely just on visual imagery.
They use radar and all sorts."

"That was Maq's point about the drone. We don't drop a

diffract meson, because we haven't got one. But we do drop something—almost any warhead would do—and we make it *look* like a diffract meson. Maq figured that Zeus could not afford to take the chance. What we drop may not damage the grid, but if what went down appeared to be a killer certainty, then Zeus would have no option but to come to heel. It has to maintain the first directive, and it can't do that if its sensors tell it that the cavity is threatened with immediate collapse."

"So what are you two cretins doing just talking about it? Get on and perform. Or do you doubt your ability to project a decent holo that far? Christ! Harry Castor could have done it in his sleep!"

"Harry Castor did everything in his sleep," said Cherry sulkily. "What do you say, Tez? Do we give it a try? Me on the weaponry and you on the projectors?"

"If Zeus has called Maq's bluff, I don't see we have anything to lose. But you handle the projectors, Cherry, and I'll handle the weapons. Because one of the things I did whilst spending my time in the weapons pod was to read the instructions."

"What instructions?" asked Cherry.

"My point entirely," said Tez.

Calculation and synchronisation of missile and image took a great deal of time, but Carli's critical appraisal of their efforts at least doubled the effectiveness of their work-rate, and in less than two hours the scheme was complete. The major complication was the capacity of the space-sweepers to catch fast-moving objects in flight, and they had to allow that at least some of their attempts would be nullified by premature interception.

This raised the point that if some of the warheads which were apparently diffract mesons produced no more than a plain nuclear reaction when stopped in flight, Zeus would still have no positive evidence that the diffract meson existed. To this end they arranged that the first missiles should appear merely larger than they actually were, but not to appear to have diffract characteristics. Only when Cherry saw the clear opportunity of getting an unintercepted missile straight down to the grid would the diffract meson hologram be used, and Tez reserved a pre-designated weapon specifically for this purpose.

Then finally everything was ready except the initiative to begin. A knowledge of the dramatic potential of the accompanying cloud of space-sweepers inhibited both men with a great dread of what might happen if things went wrong. But one thing both of them were even less prepared to face than an asteroid-gathering space machine, and that was Carli in a full flood of anger and contempt. Though their fingers tended to falter at the instant of decision, one look at her critical eyes was sufficient to convince them that there were fates worse than death.

It was therefore with a feeling something akin to relief that Tez got his first warhead away. Sound-triggered, Cherry's image started at the same time, but tended to fall behind, because of a slight miscalculation of the absolute velocity of the projectile. By the time the correction had been made, however, one of the attendant space-sweepers had swooped at the offending object with a speed and accuracy far geater than they had believed possible, and had actively clutched the missile itself when Tez decided to detonate.

Instantly, the computer screen altered to display a new message.

A PI-INVERSION FIELD IS UNAFFECTED BY NU-CLEAR EXPLOSIONS. THE EXISTENCE OF A DIF-FRACT MESON WEAPON IS STILL NOT ADMITTED.

It was Carli, however, frowning over her one-fingered typing, who gave the answer.

BUT THAT WAS ONLY FOR STARTERS, YOU HAVEN'T SEEN ANYTHING YET!

The nuclear warhead, however, did have one effect. Whilst not destroying the space-sweeper, it certainly disabled its ability to catch, and the great machine wheeled out wide so as to leave the field free for some of its companion machines.

Tez then tried a salvo of three missiles, close-spaced. Two were intercepted, with a resultant blaze of energy which blocked the *Shellback*'s screens momentarily, but the third slipped through to explode on the surface of the rim itself. As Zeus had predicted, the Exis field was unaffected, and all the radiation and destructive forces were reflected back into space, but it did give the trio in the little ship the faint hope that they could finally win, because it proved the machines of Zeus were not quite as infallible as they had been led to suppose.

Of the seven further warheads, five resulted in the retirement of the intercepting engines, and two more wasted their energies against the impenetrable field which maintained the cavity and the grid. Then Cherry saw his opportunity in a clearing of the field as new 'sweepers swung in to replace some of those incapacitated by the blasts. He signalled to Tez that the next image should carry the diffract meson image, and the die was cast.

By God and guesswork the union of image and artifact worked out perfectly. Even the crew of the *Shellback* had to gasp as the image of what was visually a diffract meson warhead sped straight towards the rim. A space-sweeper fled desperately towards it, completely miscalculated its actual size, and missed. For a moment the image was lost to them by being obscured by the 'sweeper's bulk, then it again became visible on the screens speeding like an arrow towards the slight lines on the rim which marked the feedlines to the Exis grid.

They held their breaths and hoped. As though hypnotised, Carli sat before the computer and chewed the corner of her handkerchief, willing the screen to change. For a long while the last message from Zeus held firm, then suddenly flickered and was gone. The projectile continued its true descent, and with more care and attention than he had ever applied before, Cherry corrected and nursed his holo-image to make the illusion a perfect composite. Then only a few seconds before impact the computer screen flared suddenly.

THREAT ACKNOWLEDGED AS ACTUAL. ABORT.
THE FIRST DIRECTIVE SHALL BE REVISED.

Tez cancelled the detonation of his missile probably only yards before it struck, and Cherry allowed his image to follow through to contact with the rim before disengaging the illusion. He was still not convinced that they could possibly have won, and being steeped in lifelong traditions of human duplicity, he even now expected the screen to flare with accusations of: "Liar!", "Cheat!" and "Fraud!". He had not noticed the subtlety in the syntax in which Zeus had already proclaimed by the use of "shall" that the revision of the directive was a future imperative, and therefore beyond logical reconsideration. Cherry was still prepared for the worst when the screen changed again to ask the single question:

WHEN?

It was Tez who first noticed the change outside. Slowly at first, and then with increasing rapidity, the great space-sweepers who had surrounded them were drifting away, re-grouping, and moving off into the cageworld cavity or being re-directed to other tasks far across the reaches of Hermes-space. Finally their own particular "guardian" 'sweeper was also withdrawn, and suddenly they were free to move where and how they wished.

They stood in the observation bay, watching the withdrawal of the great fleet, and still not fully understanding the true nature of the battle they had won, or the staggering weight of responsibility which had just passed back to man. The reprograming of the first directive would contribute nothing towards solving the looming population crisis which would arrive when the Solarian universe could no longer be expanded. All that Ancor had achieved was an assurance that Zeus would continue to operate all its routine functions when that point arrived. Nothing and nobody could yet answer the terrifying question: "Where will our emigrants go then?"

Perhaps there was no answer, never could be an answer, and the decisions to be made would be horrendous. Whether to allow the shells and worlds to choke themselves through overpopulation until stability was achieved through increased rates of mortality; or whether to pump the unsuspecting emigrants out into whatever strange wastes lay beyond Solaria's edge, a sacrifice of millions to sustain trillions. Or were there other places to go if the immutable laws of relativity could somehow be broken or avoided? Or even could a new Solaria be made, complete with its own internal sun? Tez and Cherry had no thoughts of this, but felt only a great relief at their own personal deliverance. The rest of the problems were locked in the brain of Maq Ancor, who twisted as if in torment in his sleep in the arms of Sine Anura.

Cherry tried the radio again, but was still unable to gain any response. They had, however, the assurance that Maq and Sine were somewhere on or in the shell of Mercury, and doubtless radio conditions would improve as the distance decreased. Cherry therefore worked out his co-ordinates for their passage across Hermes-space, and the brave little *Shellback* turned once more towards the centre of Solaria.

CHAPTER THIRTY

In High Places

"WHAT DO we do now?" asked Sine Anura.

Ancor shrugged. He had given up trying to get control of the automatic ship. Even had he been able to gain access to the right circuits, he could still not have forged them into a workable system which would have enabled him to pilot the craft. Nor, since they were desperately dependent on the ship's life-support devices, did he dare make even the most tentative experiments.

Having been conveyed to this spot to see the sun, they had expected shortly again to be lifted from the position and taken somewhere else; it was in considering where else they might be taken that Ancor realised his mistake. He had agreed to withold the use of his threat against Zeus on the condition that he and Sine were taken to see the sun. But he had forgotten also to make the arrangement conditional also on their being brought back—ever! Their own recovery was never part of the stated bargain.

They now faced the dilemma of not knowing whether Zeus regarded their return to the *Shellback* as implicit in the deal—in which case it might attempt to return them via the spoke terminal which had been the scene of so much violence—or whether it would be content to leave them in the ship for fear that it might automatically depart without them. Only Cherry and the *Shellback* offered any real prospect for getting them back alive, and the *Shellback*, as far as they were aware, was encircled by space-sweepers, and was duty-bound to remain on station until, if ever, Zeus came up with a positive reply.

Three times the sunlight rose behind the peaks, on a cycle of approximately seven day intervals, and three times they watched it regretfully through the ports, not daring to go out again. In the interim periods Ancor spent long hours at the radio, being unable to understand why it was now so poor as to be virtually useless, whereas when they had first landed he had at least been able to have a partial conversation with Cherry. He checked the power supplies most carefully, but could find nothing amiss, and he knew that the *Shellback*'s transmitters were self-correcting for optimum performance. So there had to be another factor. Apart from the occasional traces of the little ship's call signature, no form of contact could be gained, and he was beginning to have private doubts as to whether the situation could ever be improved.

The other thing which attracted his attention, for want of anything better to do, was the seven-day cycle at which they could see the sun. This was not a simple matter to resolve, it not being a straightforward function at the period of the cageworld's own revolution in the cavity, and he had to set up several theoretical models in the computer before he began to understand the curious double harmonics of the cageworld's secondary mode of movement.

Then he leaped to his feet with an oath, calling down all manner of rebukes on his own stupidity as he realised that in solving the problem of the seven-day sun cycle he had probably answered his own question about the missing radio link. From habit they stood by the ports on the seventh day and watched the luminary set and then the strange magic of the sun itself begin to rise behind the rocks . . . and that was also, and probably the only, period when a radio signal reflected but once from the cavity wall could escape through the narrow "window" available to it between the bulk of the cageworld and the rim.

From the time of that discovery they had two days to wait until they could put it to the test, but in the circumstances even a slight and distant hope was far better than no hope at all, and their spirits rose appreciably. It was a tense countdown towards the exact hour, and Ancor had fine-tuned every circuit he could get at in order to maximize their chances of making an effective contact. He knew his efforts were justified when less than a minute after the calculated time the mush picked up by his receiver straining for maximum gain was suddenly quieted by the strong, clear tones of the *Shellback*'s signature.

"Ancor calling *Shellback*. Ancor calling *Shellback*! Are you receiving me?"

"Receiving you?" Cherry's voice sounded both pleased and amused. "Maq, if you get much louder you'll be able to switch off the transmitter and just plain shout."

"Look, Cherry, I've not much time. This transmission window closes down in a little while. Somehow you've got to find a way to force the issue with Zeus."

"You're a bit late for that, Maq. We've already done it. I, Cherry . . ."

"You mean it agreed?"

"Completely. But even if I say it myself, it was a perfect masterpiece of an illusion!"

"That's marvellous! But I have to keep talking quickly before this window closes on us. We're stranded and we need you to pick us up. How long do you estimate it will take you to get here?"

"Ah! If you put the kettle on, I think we should be there for tea."

"You have to be joking! Where the devil are you?"

"Just coming in through the rim of your cageworld, Maq. You didn't give us much of a lead, but from the occasional snatches of your signal the computer was able to figure a heading."

"Thank God for that, Cherry! And in return we'll do you a favour. We'll let you make a holo of the genuine Solarian sun. Just think how Harry Castor would react to that!"

The chamber of special deputies of the Mars-shell Federation Council had its first one hundred per cent attendance since its inception. As Cherry descended from his temporary dais and acknowledged Tez and Carli in the projection box, he was given a standing ovation which literally made the roof of the vast hall ring, and which lasted for fully a quarter of an hour. Even Ancor, who had seen most of the scenes recorded both on their outgoing and equally adventurous return journey had to admit that Cherry's presentation was superb.

When the cheering and the clapping had finally died, President Layor again took the stand, but despite the enthusiasm with which the extraordinary session had been greeted, her face was still stern.

"Assassin Ancor!"

"Here, Madam President!" said Ancor rising from the guest seats where he had been seated alongside Land-a.

"Assassin Ancor, you will already have have heard the results of the deliberations of the higher senate. In view of the evidence you have laid before this and other bodies, it has been unanimously agreed that we accede to your request to seek the highest quality minds available and encourage them to devote themselves to the task of reprograming the first directive of Zeus. I am further committed to express the gratitude and admiration of those people both within and without the Federation to those of you who undertook this remarkable journey, and to Prince Awa-Ce-Land-a of Hammanite, who conceived and financed it."

"Madam President, on behalf of myself and my colleagues, I thank you for those words."

"Now we come to a more difficult matter, and one concerning law rather than opinion. Those of you who were formerly Federation citizens appear here today under a temporary amnesty necessitated by the fact that under Federation law you are all liable to criminal charges to a greater or lesser degree of seriousness. Now it is not our intention to lock up or execute the most popular figures of our time, yet the terms of the law must be satisfied. Certain proposals for a compromise solution have been made, with which I do not intend to waste the time of this assembly. I think the details can be more easily settled by a private discussion between you and I, as a result of which I can prepare a draft for consideration by the legislature.

When the equerry had departed from President Layor's suite and they were alone, Ancor leaned back in the sumptuous chair.

"How the hell did you manage to organise it, Leez?"

"Organise what?" Leez Layor, president of the Mars Shell Federation, looked incredibly innocent.

"Getting me included in Land-a's team. Even for you that must have been a rare piece of connivance. I didn't know what was going on myself."

"It was necessary you didn't know, Maq. Else you couldn't have played the part so convincingly. Of course we have spies in all the unfederated principalities, so we've known for a long time what Land-a had in mind. Not only did the Hammanites inherit a whole mountain of platinum, they also got left a stockpile of the powerplants which Zeus uses for its ultra long-range spacecraft. We couldn't force Land-a to part with any of these, so we opted for the next best thing—to have one of our own men on his team."

"But I still don't see how you induced him to pick on me?"

"We watched Land-a's attempts to build a successful team. He had the finance and he had the vital powerplant, and this meant in theory he had the means to get a ship through a cageworld interspace—which we ourselves have been trying to do for years—but it took Land-a a long while to evolve the right team for the job. As far as we know, he failed on seven previous attempts, and it was becoming quite apparent that money and mechanisms weren't the most important factors in getting through the shell. He began casting round for extremes, and we knew he needed a strong man for the lead. So we presented him with our most successful professional assassin, unfrocked and madder than a hornet. Anyone else Land-a tended to consider either got killed or compromised before the final selection was made."

"You bitch, Leez! You framed me with the Assassins' Guild."

"It wasn't difficult, Maq. There were many who were jealous of the Lion's crown."

"So what happens to Cherry and I and the others now?"

"Oh, we'll cook up something—like dual Hammanite-Federation citizenship which will give you some diplomatic immunity in both communities, and satisfy our statute books. Such things are easily arranged when you have friends in high places."

Ancor relaxed resignedly in his chair, his face lit with reluctant humour.

"Still the same old Leez! The ever-persistent schemer! That's what broke us up, isn't it? I couldn't stand being manipulated, and you couldn't resist playing puppeteer."

"Water under the bridge, Maq. Finally we both got what we wanted. I got the power, and you've the fame and the glory. All's well that ends well."

"Nothing's ended, Leez. As far as Solaria's concerned, this is only the beginning. We haven't started to unravel the mysteries and complexities of it all. Re-writing the first directive is only a palliative—something to buy us a little extra time and a chance to concern ourselves with some of the decisions. Somehow we have to look at the rest of our universe, find out what it's really like. We have to get right out to the edge and see what's beyond. We have to decide if there is a future left for man, and if so, where and how."

"I'm glad you said that, Maq," said Madam Layor. "Because it brings me to the next point I wanted to discuss. We've persuaded Land-a to let the Federation co-operate in any similar future ventures. Ajkavit University is going to become the centre for Solarian studies, whilst Land-a himself will continue to control the exploratory side. Someone is needed to coordinate the two phases, and we're in general agreement that it should be you. So what do you say to that, Director Ancor?"

"I think you're right, Leez. Sometimes it does pay to have friends in high places."

Don't miss any of these SF winners:

By JOHN BRUNNER

☐ POLYMATH (#UE1766—$2.25)
☐ INTERSTELLAR EMPIRE (#UE1668—$2.50)
☐ THE REPAIRMEN OF CYCLOPS (#UE1638—$2.25)

By M. A. FOSTER

☐ THE MORPHODITE (#UE1669—$2.75)
☐ THE GAMEPLAYERS OF ZAN (#UE1497—$2.25)
☐ THE WARRIORS OF DAWN (#UE1751—$2.50)

By PHILIP JOSÉ FARMER

☐ HADON OF ANCIENT OPAR (#UE1637—$2.50)
☐ FLIGHT TO OPAR (#UE1718—$2.50)

By SHARON GREEN

☐ THE WARRIOR WITHIN (#UE1707—$2.50)
☐ THE CRYSTALS OF MIDA (#UE1735—$2.95)

By PHILIP K. DICK

☐ FLOW MY TEARS (#UE1624—$2.25)
☐ NOW WAIT FOR LAST YEAR (#UE1654—$2.50)

By CLIFFORD D. SIMAK

☐ THE WEREWOLF PRINCIPLE (#UE1708—$2.50)
☐ THE GOBLIN RESERVATION (#UE1730—$2.25)

THE NEW AMERICAN LIBRARY, INC.,
P.O. Box 999, Bergenfield, New Jersey 07621

Please send me the DAW BOOKS I have checked above. I am enclosing
$_____ (check or money order—no currency or C.O.D.'s).
Please include the list price plus $1.00 per order to cover handling
costs.

Name _____

Address _____

City _____ State _____ Zip Code _____
Please allow at least 4 weeks for delivery